WITHDRAWN

Wishbone saw a stocky kid on roller blades headed right for him. . . .

"Look out!" Wishbone yelped.

He leaped out of the way as the boy rushed by. Then two other kids zipped past the dog.

Wishbone swallowed. "That was close," he said. But at least he was safe now.

"Wishbone!" Samantha cried. "Look out!"

The dog glanced up in time to see Samantha barreling after the ball, coming his way.

"Feet, don't fail me now!" he said.

Wishbone sprinted up onto the bleachers just as Samantha whizzed by, capturing the ball with her hockey stick.

"Don't those things come with brakes?" Wishbone asked.

***The Adventures of* WISHBONE™**
titles in Large-Print Editions:

#1 *Be a Wolf!*

#2 *Salty Dog*

#3 *The Prince and the Pooch*

#4 *Robinhound Crusoe*

#5 *Hunchdog of Notre Dame*

#6 *Digging Up the Past*

#7 *The Mutt in the Iron Muzzle*

#8 *Muttketeer!*

#9 *A Tale of Two Sitters*

#10 *Moby Dog*

The Adventures of WISHBONE™

HUNCHDOG OF NOTRE DAME

by Michael Jan Friedman

Based on the teleplay by Jack Wesley

Inspired by ***The Hunchback of Notre Dame***

by Victor Hugo

WISHBONE™ created by Rick Duffield

Gareth Stevens Publishing
MILWAUKEE

This book is a work of fiction. The characters, incidents, and dialogues are products of the author's imagination and are not to be construed as real. Any resemblance to actual events or persons, living or dead, is entirely coincidental.

For a free color catalog describing Gareth Stevens' list of high-quality books and multimedia programs, call 1-800-542-2595 (USA) or 1-800-461-9120 (Canada). Gareth Stevens Publishing's Fax: (414) 225-0377.

Library of Congress Cataloging-in-Publication Data

Friedman, Michael Jan.
Hunchdog of Notre Dame / by Michael Jan Friedman.
p. cm.
Originally published: Allen, Texas; Big Red Chair Books, © 1997.
(The adventures of Wishbone; #5)
Summary: During a fast-paced roller hockey game in which an awkward boy is humiliated by the other players, Wishbone imagines himself as Quasimodo, the hunchbacked bellringer of Paris's Notre Dame Cathedral, who defeats his enemies and saves the life of a beautiful gypsy.
ISBN 0-8368-2301-X (lib. bdg.)
[1. Dogs—Fiction. 2. Roller hockey—Fiction. 3. Physically handicapped—Fiction. 4. Notre-Dame de Paris (Cathedral)—Fiction. 5. Paris (France)—Fiction. 6. France—History—Medieval period, 987-1515—Fiction.] I. Hugo, Victor, 1802-1885. Notre-Dame de Paris. II. Title. III. Series: Adventures of Wishbone; #5.
PZ7.F8978Hu 1999
[Fic]—dc21 98-47160

This edition first published in 1999 by
Gareth Stevens Publishing
1555 North RiverCenter Drive, Suite 201
Milwaukee, Wisconsin 53212 USA

Edited by Kevin Ryan
Copy edited by Jonathon Brodman
Cover design by Lyle Miller
Interior illustrations by Arvis Stewart
Cover concept by Kathryn Yingling
Wishbone photograph by Carol Kaelson

Printed in the United States of America

1 2 3 4 5 6 7 8 9 03 02 01 00 99

For Drew,
because I said I would

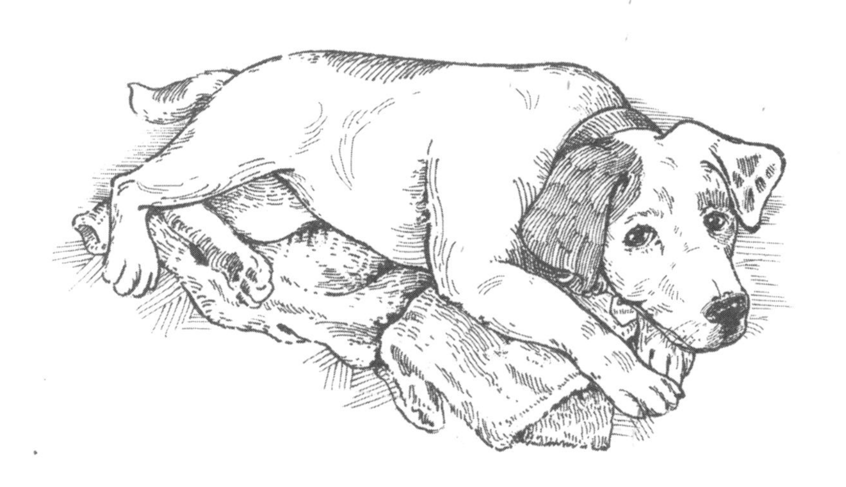

FROM THE BIG RED CHAIR . . .

Oh . . . hi! Wishbone here. You caught me right in the middle of some of my favorite things—books. Let me welcome you to my brand-new book series, THE ADVENTURES OF WISHBONE. In each of these books I have adventures with my friends in Oakdale and imagine myself as a character in one of the greatest stories of all time. In ***HUNCHDOG OF NOTRE DAME***, I imagine I'm Quasimodo, the famous bell ringer of the great Notre Dame cathedral in Paris. The story is based on the Victor Hugo novel, ***THE HUNCHBACK OF NOTRE DAME.*** It's the tale of a courageous bell ringer who everyone thinks is a monster.

You're in for a real treat, so pull up a chair and a snack and enjoy reading!

Chapter One

Wishbone entered the sunlit gymnasium of Sequoyah Middle School. He looked like a lead actor making his entrance on the stage of some majestic, new theater.

The gym was big—so big, in fact, that it took a while for the clicks of Wishbone's nails on the hardwood floor to echo off the walls and come back to him. The place smelled of several coats of varnish. There was also just a hint of the leather that covered a couple of pommel horses off in one corner.

To add to the theater effect, there were shiny, aluminum bleachers set up along each of the longer walls. Wishbone imagined the bleachers full of people, all of them eager to hear his dramatic opening line.

Unfortunately, that wouldn't happen. At that very moment, a whole pack of Wishbone's young human friends came tromping into the gym in their roller hockey gear. They were laughing and joking about the game they were about to play. Wishbone could see that they were dragging a couple of red plastic hockey goals after them.

"Hey!" said the white Jack Russell terrier with one brown ear. "Keep it down, will you? I was about to give the performance of my life here."

The kids didn't pay any attention to Wishbone. They were too excited about their roller hockey game.

Not that Wishbone could blame them. They were about to engage one another in a great struggle on the gym's varnished field of battle. They would pit speed against speed and skill against skill.

After all, they had sticks and a ball. That was all the equipment required to have a contest worthy of song and story. As far as Wishbone was concerned, they were missing just one thing, just one essential ingredient—the dog. It just so happened that he knew where they could find one.

There was only one problem. Wishbone wasn't a roller-blading kind of guy. Feet were more his kind of thing—four of 'em, to be exact. So all he could do was watch. The kids blasted back and forth across the gym floor, warming up for their chance at roller hockey glory.

Sighing, Wishbone snuffled and rested his head on his front paws. He wanted to be in the middle of the action. Center stage, as it were. That was where he really came alive.

If he couldn't take part in the game, he could still root for his favorite humans. Joe, Samantha, and David were zipping around the place in their helmets and gloves and pads. They flipped a red ball back and forth with considerable grace and accuracy.

Joe was the friendly, easygoing kid Wishbone lived with. He was also the best, most loyal friend anyone could ask for. David was the inventor in the group. He was always ready to roll up his sleeves and build an answer to any problem.

And Samantha? She was the kind of human a person just couldn't help liking—whether that person had two legs or four. Sam could find something good to say even in the worst situation.

Damont, one of Wishbone's least-favorite humans, was wheeling around the place like everyone else. Oh, sure, Damont could seem nice when he wanted to. However, he was a little too sly and slippery for Wishbone's taste. Sort of like a bone with grease all over it.

Wishbone knew the other kids as well. After all, he got around. The only kid he *didn't* know was a tall, blond boy. He'd heard Joe call the kid Nathaniel on the way to the gym.

As far as Wishbone could tell, Nathaniel seemed nice enough. A little awkward, but nice.

As Wishbone watched, Joe scooped up the ball with his stick and made an especially skillful pass. Joe was a terrific athlete. But then, Wishbone had taught Joe everything he knew.

"'Atta boy," David called.

"Real sharp," Samantha agreed.

"Bet you couldn't do it again," called Damont, always the troublemaker in the group.

"Bet he could," Sam replied.

And so on. Wishbone snorted.

He was getting frustrated with all this wheeling around. The kids had been going at it for longer than he'd expected—for several minutes, at least. By now they had to be warm enough to fry flapjacks on.

"Enough," Wishbone said. "Let the game begin."

Still, the kids insisted on skating up and down the floor. They were practicing, always practicing. Wishbone sighed. Then he jumped up onto the first row of bleachers and made himself comfortable on a nice, soft towel.

The kids whacked their red ball from one side of the gym to the other, over and over again. Wishbone tried to follow the action without getting his eyes crossed. David slammed the ball into one of the red-plastic nets the kids had set up.

"That was good," Wishbone said, trying his best to be supportive. "Real good. Sensational, in fact."

Just as he was thinking that, he saw Nathaniel

stumble and fall down. Always willing to lend a paw, Wishbone got up to go to Nathaniel's rescue. Then he stopped when he saw Samantha skate over to the boy.

"Are you okay?" she asked Nathaniel.

The boy nodded. "I'm fine."

Satisfied, Samantha skated off. As Wishbone looked on, Nathaniel got to his feet, though not as easily as some of the other kids might have. Obviously, he wasn't the most graceful human around.

In the next couple of minutes, the kids stepped up the pace. They performed tight circles, skid stops, and twisting spins. If Wishbone had been dizzy before, he was absolutely seasick now.

"Humph!" he said. "They love those wheels, don't they?"

For the life of him, he didn't understand the fascination, but he was willing to check it out. After all, he loved sticking his nose into things.

The kids continued to skate themselves silly. Wishbone made his way over to a yellow-and-black-plastic skateboard sitting near a wall. It was Samantha's. He'd seen her carry it in under her arm.

Wishbone sniffed the skateboard with disdain. Then he inspected the plastic wheels underneath it. He poked one of them with a paw.

The terrier wasn't any more impressed than before. They were just what they looked like—round things. He didn't have them, yet he got around just fine.

Standing up on his hind legs, Wishbone showed off—if only to himself.

"I mean," he said, "I play ball without wheels every day—and I'm as close to a professional as you can get. Who needs wheels to go left?"

Dropping to all fours, Wishbone faked to his left.

"To go right?"

He darted to the right.

"Or even to jump!"

He did a perfect back flip in midair.

"Try *that* with wheels," he said.

Wishbone looked around, undeniably proud of himself. But he saw no one was paying attention to him. The kids were too busy whooshing around the gym on their blades.

"Ah, well," he said. "I guess people need wheels because they've got to make do with only two feet—not four, like some fortunate souls around here." He

blew air out of his nose. "Must be tough being a human."

Just then, a stocky kid named Tommy headed right for him, skating as fast as he could. He was concentrating too hard on receiving a pass to see where he was going.

"Look out!" Wishbone yelped.

He leaped out of the way as the boy rushed by. Then two other kids zipped past the dog, trying to catch up with Tommy.

Wishbone swallowed. "That was close," he said.

But at least he was safe now . . . or so he imagined.

"Wishbone!" Samantha cried. "Look out!"

He glanced up just in time to see Samantha barreling after the ball, coming his way. Apparently, in escaping the first danger, he'd put himself right in the path of another one.

"Feet, don't fail me now!" he said.

Wishbone sprinted up onto the bleachers just as Samantha whizzed by. She captured the ball with her stick, then dished off to David, who in turn flicked a pass to Joe. The three of them moved smoothly and efficiently, like a well-oiled machine.

"Don't those things come with brakes?" Wishbone asked. His tongue was hanging out as he tried to catch his breath.

Then he realized what was happening. Joe, David, and Samantha were practicing their favorite play—the one that baffled opponents for miles around. With the ball on his stick, Joe skated toward the goal as hard as he could.

The goalie braced himself, blocking the goal mouth as best he could. Damont and another player came in to help stop Joe's shot.

But he didn't *take* a shot. At the last possible moment, he veered off to the right. Then he flipped the ball back to Samantha, who was skating just a few feet behind him.

The play worked like a charm. The goalie and the two defenders followed Joe to the side . . . leaving the net wide open for Samantha. She let go with a mighty swat and watched the ball sail into the goal.

"Beautiful," Wishbone said. "Just beautiful."

Joe and David celebrated with their friend, exchanging hugs and high-fives. Obviously, they were pretty excited.

"Great pass, Joe," Samantha told him.

"Thanks," Joe said. "It was an awesome play all around."

David nodded approvingly. "I'd say this team is ready to play some serious hockey."

Samantha's eyes lit up at the prospect. "I agree!"

They exchanged high-fives again. Damont wheeled up, a sour expression on his face. Nothing new there, Wishbone thought.

"Awright, enough talk," Damont said. "Let's choose up sides and play the game for real."

"Sure," Joe replied.

"You and I will be captains," Damont decided. "Like always."

As Wishbone watched, Joe and Damont began to select their teammates. "Aha!" he said, his ears perking up. "Now, *this* is something I can get into. The age-old ritual of choosing up sides. The process of natural selection to see who's the pick of the litter."

Damont went first. "I got Colby!" he exclaimed. Colby was a big kid with a dark-haired crew cut.

"I'll take David," Joe said.

With Damont's next turn, he picked Tina. She was small and a little fragile-looking, but really quick on her feet.

"Samantha," said Joe.

"Tommy," said Damont.

"Brett."

"Anthony."

"Drew."

The selection of teammates continued. Finally, everyone's name had been called. "There's just one exception," Wishbone noted.

Who was the runt of the litter? The last kid available?

All eyes fell on Nathaniel. The boy gulped nervously. No doubt he felt a little queasy. He knew everyone else had been chosen before him.

It was Damont's turn to pick. He took one look at Nathaniel and let out a disgusted snort. "I'm not taking him," Damont announced firmly. "No way."

Joe frowned. "Come on, Damont, you need another guy."

Damont eyed Nathaniel again—and he shook his head. "We'll make do with who we've got already."

Joe sighed, getting a little annoyed. "Damont . . ."

Nathaniel was getting more nervous with each passing comment. The tension didn't help him at all, since he was wobbly on his skates already. Wishbone could smell the anxiety. His heart went out to the kid.

"Look," Damont told Joe, "if you want Nathaniel to play so much, why don't *you* take him?"

Joe hesitated. He looked at David, then Samantha.

"Go ahead," Samantha said. "Take Nathaniel. I'll sit out for a while so he can play."

The suggestion caught Joe by surprise. "Uh-uh. You, me, and David . . . we're a team, remember?"

"Right," David chimed in. "We *always* play together."

Damont rolled his eyes. "Gab, gab, gab. Would you make up your minds already . . . while we're still young enough to skate?"

Nathaniel held his hands up. He looked fearful of creating a scene. "Look," he said, "we can just forget the whole thing."

"That's not right," Samantha said, rolling forward to come to his defense. "Nathaniel wants to play—and he *should* play."

Nathaniel was getting more and more wobbly on his skates as his nervousness increased. He tried again to back out gracefully.

"No, really. I don't mind. I don't want to start any problems."

Damont was losing his patience—not that he had a whole lot of it to begin with. "Hey, guys!" he said to Joe and his friends. "Are you going to take the dude, or what?"

"No," Nathaniel insisted. "It's okay, really."

Obviously, he was more eager than ever to end this embarrassing discussion. But as he took a step, his wobbling got worse.

Suddenly, his wheels found a life of their own. Nathaniel's legs churned to keep up with them. His arms whirled around him like helicopter blades.

He pitched forward.

Then backward.

Then forward again.

And finally fell on his back. He lay stretched out on the gym floor as if he'd suddenly decided to take a nap there.

"Ouch!" Wishbone said. "That had to hurt."

But the kids didn't express their sympathies. Instead, they began to laugh at Nathaniel. Even Joe and David snickered, although they clamped their hands over their mouths to try to hold their amusement in.

It wasn't that anyone was happy that Nathaniel had taken a tumble. They just couldn't help themselves.

Samantha was the only one who didn't seem to find Nathaniel's predicament the least bit funny. Her mouth was a tight, straight line.

Nathaniel didn't seem to see her. All he saw was the other kids. The look on his face was one of absolute devastation.

That made Damont and some of the others laugh even harder.

"Y'know," Wishbone said, "the kid's fall had to hurt, all right. But his friends' laughing at him must hurt even more."

Nathaniel sat up and stared at the kids. The laughing subsided. Joe, Sam, and David began to feel bad about what had just happened. Wishbone could tell by the embarrassed looks on their faces.

Still, the damage had been done.

"Public humiliation," he said. "There's nothing worse than that. It's sort of like what Quasimodo had to put up with."

Quasimodo, of course, was the main character in a book called *The Hunchback of Notre Dame*. It was written more than a hundred years ago by a French author named Victor Hugo.

In the story, Quasimodo's job was to ring the bells in a big, stately church known as the cathedral of Notre Dame. Unfortunately, being a bell ringer all his life had made the poor guy a little deaf—but that wasn't the worst of his problems. He was also a misshapen fellow with a hump on his back.

Not that any of that was Quasimodo's fault. Not by a long shot. After all, he was born that way. If anyone had taken the time and effort to get to know him, they would have discovered that he was as loyal, devoted, and loving on the inside as he was odd-looking on the outside.

His story takes place in 1482, in the city of Paris, France. . . .

Chapter Two

Closing his eyes, Wishbone imagined that *he* was Quasimodo, the hunchbacked bell ringer of Notre Dame.

He saw himself sitting in the great church's lofty bell tower, dressed in simple woolen clothes and a tattered cap. He was surrounded by enormous, strange-looking statues of men and animals called gargoyles.

If one didn't look too closely, one might have thought Quasimodo was a gargoyle, too. But he wasn't, of course. He was made of flesh and blood, like anyone else.

He knew that because he could feel things. He could feel joy, for instance, when he saw the sun rise, or when little birds came to eat the crumbs he laid out for them. He could feel fear when he was threatened, though he was very brave for the most part.

But the thing Quasimodo felt most often was loneliness. . . .

At that particular moment, the hunchback felt lonelier than ever. From his perch high up in the bell tower, he surveyed the square below him. Spreading out hundreds of feet from the bottom of the mighty cathedral, the large open space was jammed with people from one end to the other. There was music and dancing and laughter. A lot of brightly colored tents were set up.

It was a festival—a big public party. It was called the Day of Kings, but it was also known as the Feast of Fools.

"Two holidays for the price of one," Quasimodo said. "Quite a bargain."

The people down in the square seemed to be enjoying one another's antics. Some of them juggled colored balls in the air. Some walked through the crowd stiff-legged on tall stilts. Others ate fire—not really, of course, but it certainly looked real. Still others sang songs on rickety wooden stages, while pipers piped their melodies in accompaniment.

"I'd like to join the party, too," Quasimodo said.

He wanted to sing and dance and make merry like everyone else. But the bell ringer didn't have much of a voice to sing. He also wasn't very graceful as a dancer, with a big old hump on his back.

Quasimodo wasn't the only one who wanted to take part in the festival. After all the time he'd spent in Notre Dame's bell tower, Quasimodo had come to think of the tall, stately looking cathedral as his friend. He felt he knew what it was thinking. Right at that moment, he felt it would have loved to sing along with the pipers.

The hunchback looked at the cathedral bells hanging from their thick, wooden beams, as silent and forlorn as he was. He felt sad for them. Suddenly, he had a whopper of an idea.

Leaping into the air, he used his teeth to catch hold of one of the ropes that were attached to the bells. Then, his four legs churning for balance, he swung across the open space where the bells resided.

The bell made a loud, happy clang, finally able to take part in the merriment down below. When Quasimodo swung back the other way, the bell clanged again, even louder.

In mid-swing, the hunchback let go of the rope and clamped onto another one. That made one of the other bells sing, this time in a deeper voice. But it seemed just as thrilled to join the party as the first bell did.

Quasimodo went on like that for a good three or four minutes, swinging from rope to rope, waking bell

after bell, until they were all booming and chiming in a joyous chorus.

Then he leaped back to the cold floor where he lived and ate and slept. He landed on his paws and watched as the bells swung back and forth. It made his tail wag with delight.

"There," he said. "The cathedral got its wish. It's singing along with everyone down below now."

It made Quasimodo feel pretty good. But as he turned and gazed down on the people in the square, he began to consider something even better.

"I need to get out more," he said with a snort. "I can't spend my whole life in a tower. It's just not healthy."

But he didn't dare to join the party—or did he?

In the bell tower, he was nice and safe. No one bothered him there. He had food and shelter and a wonderful view of the city, with the blue and orange rooftops and elegant towers.

In the square, though . . . that would be quite a different story. Quasimodo wasn't used to being among people. He had no way of knowing how they would react to him.

Still, he was *so* lonely, and the party looked like so much fun. With all that was going on down there, the merrymakers might not even notice that the hunchback was among them.

Jumping up onto the low stone wall that encircled

the tower, Quasimodo took a deep breath and leaped. A moment later, he landed on a rough ledge that stuck out from the building only a few inches.

It was a trick only he could have pulled off. A regular person would have missed the ledge and fallen to his death. Quasimodo, however, was much more agile than anyone else he had ever seen.

"So far, so good," he said.

Then he leaped again, onto another ledge. And another. And so on and so on. He landed on his paws each time, until the ground was only a scant dozen feet away.

Bunching his four legs beneath him, he soared one last time—and headed for the crowded square below. His paws met the cobblestones with a jolt. Wagging his tail with anticipation, he raised his snout and gave a quick sniff around.

What he smelled was a little frightening. Quasimodo had never been in such a big, tightly packed crowd before. He had never sniffed so many strong smells: the tart scent of fresh apples; the earthy odor of roasted potatoes; the sweet smell of ale.

The hunchback had occasionally caught a whiff of these aromas from afar, but never up close. It was an exciting experience, to say the least.

Quasimodo was so wrapped up in the exotic sights and the smells of the place that he forgot other people could see *him*. However, a man with yellowed teeth, one of the noisiest of all the people assembled there, pointed to Quasimodo as he walked through the forest of legs.

"Look!" he cried out. "Here he comes!"

Quasimodo looked around. "Here *who* comes?" he wondered.

"It's the Prince of Fools!" cried a man wearing an eye patch. "Let's give him a throne. And a crown!"

"Yes," Quasimodo agreed. "Let's do that." But he still didn't know who these people were talking about.

Then the hunchback saw everyone staring in his direction. He finally realized they were talking about *him*. Before he knew it, some of the men in the crowd had taken a soft little platform with handles out of one of the tents. They picked Quasimodo up by the scruff of his neck and plunked him down on top of the platform.

A moment later, someone else put something on his head and on his shoulders. The object on his head was a red dunce's cap with bells hanging from it. The thing on his shoulders was an elegant-looking cape. It was so threadbare, however, that Quasimodo's fur showed through in a number of places. All in all, he thought, he must have looked pretty silly.

But that was exactly the idea, wasn't it? He, Quasimodo, had apparently been picked to be the festival's King of Fools.

Four men lifted his little platform on their broad shoulders and paraded him through the square. His tail wagging, the bell ringer had to admit he kind of liked the experience. It was nice to get so much attention from people he'd never met before. Actually, it was nice to get attention from *anybody.*

Quasimodo looked up to the great, gray-stone cathedral, which had always sheltered him from the world. He expected it to seem proud of him, to look happy that he'd found friends among the common people.

But the cathedral didn't look happy at all. It looked worried for him. It seemed to tell him that attention was good sometimes . . . but that this was the *wrong* kind of attention.

Then the hunchback heard the cruel laughter of the crowd and saw the faces people were making at him—and he realized the cathedral was right. These commoners weren't his friends at all. They were just making fun of him, holding him up to ridicule for their own amusement.

He lowered his head, and his tail stopped wagging.

"Wait," he said. "This wasn't exactly what I had in mind when I said I wanted to get out more."

Quasimodo tried to get down from his fool's throne. The men holding him didn't give him a chance. They just laughed and lifted the hunchback high above the crowd, so everyone could see how ridiculous he looked.

"Why," said a tall man, sounding disappointed, "that's no king. It's just Quasimodo, the bell ringer!"

"Ugh!" a woman grunted with disgust. "The hunchback!"

"You know," another man added, "he lives way up in the cathedral's bell tower, all by himself."

The woman smiled a gap-toothed smile. "At least when he's up there, we don't have to set eyes on that awful hump!"

"All right, all right," Quasimodo barked, his fur bristling with embarrassment. "You've made your point! Now get me down from here!"

But the people didn't let him down. They paraded him around the square and made fun of him some more. They laughed and pointed at him, and they remarked loudly about his deformity.

Suddenly, their heads all turned at once. Quasimodo sniffed the air. There was a new scent in the area. It was a very *pleasant* scent, too, like the sweetest and most fragrant of flowers.

His ears perking up, the hunchback heard a melody he'd never heard before—a lovely, haunting little tune. A moment later, the crowd parted—and revealed a slender girl with colorful ribbons in her long, dark hair. She was singing and dancing and playing the tambourine.

She was the most beautiful, most graceful being Quasimodo had ever seen. With each note she sang, her dark eyes flashed. The bell ringer couldn't help but stare openmouthed at her. Neither could anyone else, he noticed.

"Wow!" Quasimodo said softly, his tail wagging as if it had a will of its own. "Who is that? She's more beautiful than a bowl full of nice, juicy bones."

The hunchback would find out later that her name was Esmeralda. She was a Gypsy. That meant her people didn't have any homeland of their own. They were, in a way, like stray dogs. They wandered from one place to another, making a living on their charm and ability to entertain.

The Gypsies hadn't always lived in France, of course. They originally lived in an exotic, faraway place called India. Eventually, they had made the long journey west to the continent of Europe in search of a better life for themselves.

As Esmeralda danced, people just couldn't keep their eyes off her. They weren't gazing at her mockingly, the way they'd looked at the hunchback on his fool's throne. They eyed her with admiration.

The Gypsy didn't give any sign that she noticed all their attention. Her eyelids fluttered as she dipped and whirled. She was too caught up in the sheer joy of movement to be aware of much that was going on around her.

Then her gaze fell on Quasimodo—and she came to a complete stop in her dance routine. Her eyes widened and her mouth opened, but no words came out. But the look on her face told the bell ringer exactly what she was feeling.

Disgusted, even a little frightened, she turned away from him. Then she glanced over her shoulder at him again.

"Uh . . . hi," Quasimodo said timidly.

What else *could* he say? The look in the Gypsy's eyes told him she wasn't eager to have a long conversation with him.

"Hey!" some smart aleck in the crowd yelled out. "Look at this, my friends!" He pointed to Esmeralda, then to Quasimodo. "We've got the Beauty . . . and the Beast!"

Everyone laughed—everyone except the hunchback and Esmeralda. Struck with fear, the Gypsy ran away, darting through the crowd.

Quasimodo watched her disappear. "Who am I to compare to her beauty?" he asked with a sigh.

Just then, someone else appeared—someone the bell ringer knew very well. The fellow had a little puff of gray hair sticking out from beneath his hat. He wore beautiful, gray-velvet robes. And he seemed angry that Quasimodo's foolish appearance had put an end to the girl's dancing.

His name was Dom Claude Frollo, a priest who had an important position in the Church. He was also the hunchback's master—the man who had fed and

clothed the bell ringer since his birth, and had given him his job high up in the bell tower.

Grabbing Quasimodo's silly hat, Dom Frollo threw it to the ground. Then he tied a leash around the bell ringer's neck.

"Uh-oh," Quasimodo said. "I don't like leashes—no, sir."

Dom Frollo didn't seem to care. Snatching the hunchback off the little platform, Dom Frollo plopped him onto the ground.

"Whoa!" Quasimodo said. "Take it easy, okay? Handle with care, if you don't mind!"

Dom Frollo started to wave his arms and make hand signals at the hunchback. After all, the man knew Quasimodo's sense of hearing wasn't all that it could be.

Still, it wasn't as if he couldn't hear *at all*.

"Um . . . sir," Quasimodo said formally, "I may be a little deaf, and that may be sign language, but you've got quite a stutter."

Dom Frollo's eyes blazed at him. "Don't play cute with me," he threatened. "You know who I am. Surely you haven't forgotten how I took you in when you were left as an orphaned pup on the steps of the cathedral. Remember how I raised you, taught you everything you know?"

"How could I have forgotten?" Quasimodo asked. "You remind me of it every day."

His master made a face and tugged on his leash. "Come, Quasimodo, we have no time for this foolishness. We have important work to do."

"Important work?" Quasimodo wondered. "What could that be?"

As Dom Frollo turned and made his way through the crowd, the bell ringer followed. But he had the distinct feeling that what his master had in mind was *not* a good thing.

Chapter Three

That evening, two mysterious figures made their way through the dark, winding streets of Paris, weaving in and out of the shadows. One walked on two legs, the other on four.

The two-legged figure was Dom Claude Frollo. The four-legged one was Quasimodo.

Dom Frollo led the way, scurrying across the cobblestones in his fine robes. The hunchback padded along behind him, the stones hard and rough under his soft paws. Finally, Dom Frollo saw the entrance to a tavern.

With a gesture to the bell ringer, Dom Frollo went inside. Quasimodo walked behind him, following the smoothness of the wooden boards. Stepping on wood was a welcome change after all those hard cobblestones.

The hunchback had never been inside a tavern

before. It was packed with loud people, and even louder music. They were cheering someone or something at the far end of the room, over by a roaring fire in a great stone fireplace.

Quasimodo sniffed the smoky air and picked out a familiar scent. It was sweet and fragrant.

"It smells like flowers," he said, his tail wagging merrily.

Even before Dom Frollo led him through the crowd to get a better view, Quasimodo knew who the scent belonged to. Unless his nose was playing tricks on him, it was Esmeralda the people were cheering.

Sure enough, when Dom Frollo and Quasimodo made their way to the front of the crowd, they saw her. She was swaying and whirling the same way she had danced in the square by Notre Dame cathedral. The firelight seemed to gleam in her hair.

People were tossing shiny coins at Esmeralda's feet to show their appreciation for her performance. The coins clinked on the wooden floor and glinted in the light from the fire.

Dom Frollo found a table and sat down. The hunchback sat beside him, his tail still wagging. He waited for his master to say or do something. Dom Frollo just stared at the beautiful Gypsy girl—and looked as if he were in pain.

"So," Quasimodo said, "what's for dinner tonight,

boss?" The hunchback always focused on the most important things first! Then he looked around. "Who does a fella have to know around here to see a menu?"

"Look at her," Dom Frollo said breathlessly, still staring at Esmeralda. "Her eyes are as black and sparkling as the night. Her feet flow together like spokes in a spinning wheel. Her graceful arms twine and entwine like two silk scarves. . . ." His voice trailed off into silence.

Suddenly, the hunchback realized what was happening. "I get it," he said. "You like her, right, boss? Like a girlfriend, I mean."

Dom Frollo's hands clenched into fists, his eyes narrowing. "I must have her. I *must.*" He turned to his companion. "And you will get her for me."

"Me?" Quasimodo asked, feeling a chill run down his spine, right to the end of his tail. "But—"

"You," his master insisted.

Dom Frollo was so in love with the Gypsy that he looked ill. His face was pale, and there were dark circles under his eyes. All this, and he and the bell ringer had been in the tavern only a couple of minutes.

"Oooh," said Quasimodo, rolling his eyes, "my master is—how shall I say this?—*extremely* troubled."

Dom Frollo didn't seem to find the humor in the remark. Standing suddenly, he bent over the hunchback and showed Quasimodo his fist. It was pretty big, as fists went.

"You will get her for me," he said menacingly. "Or else."

The bell ringer gulped. "On the other hand, you're a reasonably attractive man with only partial male-pattern baldness—and you've still got all your teeth, right? Well, most of them, anyway. So what's not to like?"

"Indeed," Dom Frollo agreed, his features softening ever so slightly.

"Heh! Heh!" Quasimodo laughed. But inside, he was thinking, *Oh, boy, this isn't a job for a bell ringer. It's a job for a magician.*

Fortunately, a plan was beginning to take shape in his ever-so-fertile imagination.

Later on that night, Esmeralda left the tavern in a braided shawl. She moved alone through the rain-slick streets of Paris. At least, she probably *thought* she was alone. However, she had a hunchback on her trail.

In other words, Quasimodo. The bell ringer had a mission to carry out for his master, Dom Frollo.

After a while, seeing she hadn't noticed he was following her, Quasimodo decided to make his move. Approaching her over the cobblestones, the hunchback cleared his throat. After all, he didn't want to startle her.

Esmeralda was startled anyway. She whirled, aware now that there was someone behind her. Her eyes widened when she saw the hunchback.

"It's just me," Quasimodo said, hoping to calm her down. He was wagging his tail, and he had a coin in his mouth—one of those that had been thrown to her in the tavern. "Here," he told her. "You forgot one of your tips."

Staring at him, the Gypsy took the coin. But she didn't speak.

"Blech!" the hunchback said, glad to get the coin out of his mouth. "Thanks. Tasty, it wasn't."

Quasimodo looked at Esmeralda, seeing how her eyes shone in the moonlight. She was a work of art, all right. He could see why Dom Frollo was falling in love with her.

To tell the truth, *he* was starting to feel a little something for the Gypsy himself.

"Now, listen to me," the bell ringer told her. "I know this is going to sound crazy, but there's this guy who wants to meet you. He's my friend and . . . well, actually, he's my master . . ." He took a deep breath and put his thoughts in order. "Okay, actually, he's totally nuts—about you, that is."

Esmeralda didn't seem to be very interested in meeting Dom Frollo. "I must be going," she said politely, and she started to leave.

"No, wait," Quasimodo told her. He leaped up on

his hind legs with alarm. "You don't understand, Miss. If you don't say *bonjour*—hello—to my friend, it's *au revoir*—good-bye—for yours truly. I hope you catch my meaning."

The Gypsy tilted her head to one side. *"Au revoir?"* she repeated. "For you? You mean you're in—"

Suddenly, the hunchback saw a pair of hands reach out of the shadows, seeking Esmeralda. She noticed it, too—and she screamed in fear. Then she fainted and fell to the ground.

As Quasimodo rushed over to her, Dom Frollo stepped out of the shadows. His eyes were wild, like a crazy person's.

"What did you do to her?" the hunchback asked.

Frollo's head turned, as if he'd heard something. "I must escape." He breathed heavily. Then he moved back into the shadows he had come from.

"What?" said Quasimodo. "I mean . . . hey, come back here! Hey, boss!"

But it was no use. Dom Frollo vanished into the black of night. Then the hunchback, whose hearing wasn't as good as his master's, began to hear what Frollo had heard.

It was the sound of approaching footsteps. Someone was coming. In fact, it seemed to be a whole bunch of someones.

Still, Quasimodo's only concern was for poor Esmeralda. He leaned close to her, sniffing her face.

"Um . . . Miss . . . Miss," he said, "wake up, please. You're all right, aren't you? Tell me you're all right."

Suddenly, the hunchback found himself surrounded by a bunch of legs in leather boots—the kind that belonged to the city guards. He looked all the way up at their faces. Judging by their expressions, they weren't very happy to see him.

"You there!" one of the guards snarled at him.

Quasimodo grinned nervously, showing them his teeth. "Oh . . . uh . . . hi, guys. Top of the evening to you." He looked around at them. "Would you believe me if I told you this isn't what it looks like?"

The guards didn't answer. They just glared at him.

"I didn't think so," the hunchback said softly.

Then they snatched him up roughly and carried him away. Quasimodo didn't know what the punishment for kidnapping was, but he was sure it would turn out to be a doozy. . . .

Chapter Four

Wishbone was still dreaming about Quasimodo's troubles when he sniffed a familiar scent. Opening his eyes, he saw that he was still in the school gymnasium in Oakdale. Damont was staring down at him just like one of the city guards in Paris.

"Wishbone!" Damont said.

Damont didn't sound happy at all. But for the life of him, Wishbone couldn't figure out why.

"What?" he said. "I'm nowhere near your game, right? So what's the problem?"

Damont scowled. "Get off my towel, will ya?"

Wishbone looked down and realized he'd been snoozing on Damont's towel. It had certainly felt more comfortable than the hard bleacher seats.

"Fine," Wishbone said. "Take it." Getting up, he walked away. "Sheesh! There had to be a nicer way to say that."

Damont snatched up the towel and wiped his face with it. Then he returned to the action on the court. Wishbone saw that the two teams the kids had selected before were in the thick of a ferocious blade hockey game.

There, in the thickest of the thick, was none other than Nathaniel.

"Guess the kid got his chance," the dog said. "Good for him."

As Wishbone watched, the two teams skated back and forth. Finally, Joe and Samantha worked that special play of theirs. Joe rocketed toward their opponent's goal, drawing the attention of the goalie and two of Damont's biggest teammates.

"Watch out for Samantha!" Damont cried out, too far way himself to do anything about it. "For Samantha!"

But his teammates either didn't hear him or they

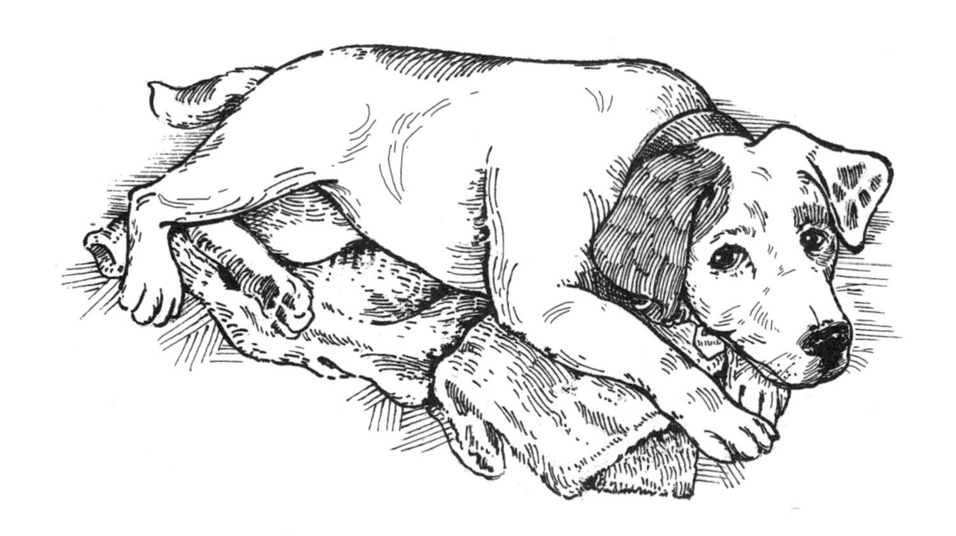

couldn't respond in time. When Joe veered off to the left, they went with him.

Like clockwork, Joe shot the ball back to Sam. Just as before, she sent it skidding into the net.

"Score!" said Wishbone.

"One to nothing!" Joe cried out.

"Not for long!" Damont shouted back.

A few seconds later, the boy got a chance to make good on his boast. One of Damont's teammates stole the ball and passed it to him at midcourt.

With a quick move, Damont got past David and into the clear. Then he veered to the right to get an angle and slapped the ball at the goal as hard as he could.

Joe's goalie gave it his best shot, but he didn't stand a chance. Damont was known for the speed and accuracy of his slapshot. Sure enough, the ball shot right between the goalie's knee pads, tying up the game.

"One all," Damont said.

"We'll get another chance," Samantha assured Joe.

"Yes," said David. "This isn't over yet by a long shot."

Wishbone wagged his tail. "Such drama!" he said. "Such tragedy! Such courage!" He couldn't wait to see the rest of the game.

A few seconds later, Damont's team got the ball again. Skating backward, their eyes on their opponents, Joe and his teammates prepared to defend their goal.

As the ball whizzed to Damont, Joe stuck his stick out and broke up the pass. The ball skittered away, heading more or less for Nathaniel. He hadn't really gotten involved in the action until then.

Nathaniel lunged for the ball, but missed. In the process, he lost his balance—just as he had when the kids were choosing sides.

Arms flailing, Nathaniel staggered into Joe. Joe tried to hold them both up, but the effort was too much for him. A moment later, they fell together in a tangle of arms and legs.

"Then again," Wishbone said wistfully, "maybe the drama will have to wait a while."

Joe sighed and got to his feet. Nathaniel tried to get up the same way, but he only managed to flop to the floor again.

Wishbone cocked his head. "Looks like I'm not the only one around here who doesn't belong on wheels."

Damont and his teammates began to laugh at Nathaniel again. His face reddening with embarrassment, the boy lurched this way and that. Finally, he managed to stand up on his skates. But that was the moment Damont chose to whiz by him, in a rush to retrieve the ball.

Damont didn't bump into Nathaniel. He didn't even brush against him. But that didn't matter. Nathaniel reacted as if Damont *was* going to hit him.

In other words, he threw all his weight in the opposite direction. The result? A wild spin, a split, and . . . *flomp!* Poor Nathaniel hit the floor all over again.

"Oh, yeah," Wishbone said. "I've got to have a talk with this kid right away, before he ends up in the hospital."

But Nathaniel was persistent. Wishbone had to say that much for him. He did his best to push himself up off the floor again. At last he succeeded.

Collecting the ball with his stick, Damont winked at his teammates. "Hey, check this out!" he said.

Wishbone looked at him, wondering what the Damonster had in mind. Suddenly, he thought he knew. But it was already too late for Wishbone to do anything about it.

Damont glided toward Nathaniel, who was still struggling to get to his feet. Before Nathaniel could straighten up, Damont cut a circle around him on his skates. Then he cut another, and another, until Nathaniel was too dizzy to see straight.

"Damont!" Wishbone said. "Of all the nasty tricks!"

Nathaniel started to fall this way, then that. Finally, the boy collapsed to the floor in a big, woozy heap.

Damont laughed. So did the other players on his team.

Nathaniel could only sit there, humiliated. He

knew he looked like an idiot—Wishbone could see it in his eyes. Embarrassed for him, the dog held his paws over his face.

"Boy," he said, "this kid can't catch a break."

Suddenly, a pair of hands reached for Nathaniel. Wishbone looked up and saw that they belonged to Samantha.

"Here," she said gently, "I'll help you up."

And she did. She worked carefully, so Nathaniel wouldn't lose his footing again. A moment later, he was on his feet.

Samantha smiled at Nathaniel. For the first time that day, the boy's eyes brightened a little. A grin spread across his face—and it was all thanks to Sam's kindness.

Wishbone wagged his tail. "Now, there's somebody with the courage to offer a helping hand," he said, "even when it might not be such a popular thing to do."

Chapter Five

Back in Paris, Quasimodo the hunchback was in need of a helping hand, too.

He was standing wrapped in heavy, iron chains in the square in front of Notre Dame cathedral. His paws and head were locked up tight so he couldn't get away. The chains rubbed against his soft fur. They were extremely uncomfortable for him, especially on such a hot and steamy day.

To make matters even worse, the bell ringer was forced to stand on a slowly turning wooden platform. The purpose of the revolving platform was to give everyone in the crowd a good look at him.

The situation was humiliating for Quasimodo, to say the least. It was even more humiliating than being crowned King of Fools the day before. The people around him, troublemakers all, teased the hunchback and laughed at his misfortune until their sides ached.

Quasimodo definitely needed some assistance. He'd been accused of a crime he hadn't committed.

Squinting in the bright sunlight, the bell ringer could see his friends the gargoyles high up near the bell tower. They seemed to see his misery, but there was nothing they could do about it. The gargoyles were only pieces of carved stone, silent and helpless—as helpless as Quasimodo himself.

One of the bigger fellows in the crowd came up to jeer at the unfortunate bell ringer. "So, Quasimodo, how do you like your punishment for trying to kidnap that poor, defenseless Gypsy girl?"

A woman with a mole on her face came up to accuse Quasimodo, too. "You were thinking you could woo her with your good looks, maybe? If that's so, you're a bigger fool than we thought!"

Quasimodo needed these insults like he needed another tail. But what could he do? He was stuck there.

The cruelty of the crowd was nothing compared to the misery caused by the blazing sun. It was really taking its toll on the hunchback, making him feel overheated and light-headed. He panted with a terrible thirst, his long, pink tongue hanging out.

"Please," he said, gasping, "may I have some water? Just a little?" He looked around. "Someone? Anyone?"

The man who had been making fun of him pushed the woman with the mole at him. As she stumbled forward, her face stopped right in front of Quasimodo's. Startled, she screamed.

"Mam'zelle would love to get you some cool water," the guy said with a chuckle, "if you give her a nice smooch."

The woman swatted at the man. "Get me away from the hunchbacked brute!" she yelled, obviously scared to death of Quasimodo.

Twisting out of the man's grasp, she ran away. Suddenly, a deep, low murmur shot through the crowd. A second later, the bell ringer saw why.

It was Esmeralda, the beautiful Gypsy. She was shouldering her way to the front of the crowd, her eyes fixed on Quasimodo.

"Let me through," she said. "Please, let me through."

"Uh-oh," said the bell ringer, his tail wagging with anticipation—and not the good kind. "Bad news. She must hate me for what she thinks I did to her."

Slowly, Esmeralda approached Quasimodo. When she got close enough, her lively dark eyes studied his sad face. Then she reached behind her back for something.

"This is it," he said, his eyes opening wide. "The Gypsy girl wants revenge! I'm doomed—and I mean *big*-time!"

Fearing the worst, the hunchback pulled away as far as he could—which wasn't far at all, thanks to the heavy chains wrapped around his body. As it turned out, however, his fears were all for nothing.

It wasn't a knife Esmeralda was holding. "In fact," he said, "it isn't a weapon at all."

It was a clay gourd full of water. As Quasimodo watched, the Gypsy girl poured some out onto the wooden platform. He couldn't believe it.

"What?" he said with great surprise. "Water? You? Me? Wow!"

He lapped up the water with this thirsty tongue. Then she poured him some more. The crowd grumbled menacingly at her.

"I wouldn't do that if I was you," the man with yellowed teeth snarled. "It's not very smart."

The mole-faced woman who had been pushed at Quasimodo said, "He's the work of the devil, dearie. Don't you know that? He's as wicked as he is misshapen."

Fortunately for Quasimodo, Esmeralda ignored the people in the crowd. She continued to pour water for him. Of course, he kept on lapping it up as fast as she could pour.

"Thanks," he told her, in between gulps. "I mean, really thanks. I mean, really, really, really thanks."

"I felt sorry for you." Esmeralda sighed, emptying the last drops of water on the platform. "What else could I have done?"

"You could have ignored me, the way everyone else did," he said. "But you didn't. You helped."

Esmeralda smiled at Quasimodo. It was a beautiful smile, maybe the most beautiful thing he had ever seen. Little by little, he could feel his bruised bell ringer's heart melting for her.

Chapter Six

Suddenly, Wishbone realized he'd been day-dreaming again. He wasn't really in the square outside Notre Dame cathedral, accepting water from a beautiful Gypsy girl named Esmeralda.

He was in the gym, where the kids were playing, watching Samantha pull Nathaniel toward the door.

"Come on," she said, "let's go."

Nathaniel was stunned. "Huh? What do you mean?"

Samantha didn't answer. She just continued to pull Nathaniel toward the exit. But Joe came over and stopped her.

"Where are you going?" he asked.

Samantha shrugged her shoulders. "I'm going to teach Nathaniel how to skate."

Joe was shocked. "You're *what?*"

"She's *what?*" Wishbone echoed.

Nathaniel was more shocked than any of them. "You're *what?*"

Damont skated up to Samantha. "You're kidding, right?" He indicated Nathaniel with a tilt of his head. "The kid's a total klutz! He couldn't skate if he had *twenty* legs!"

Samantha turned red and went nose to nose with Damont. "Oh," she said. "Like you've never fallen down or embarrassed yourself in public before? Nathaniel just needs some lessons, that's all."

She turned briskly to face Nathaniel.

"That is, of course, if you *want* me to help you," Sam said to her newfound friend.

No doubt, the kid couldn't believe what he was hearing. "Well . . . yes. I mean . . . sure I do."

Samantha smiled. "Okay, then. Let's go."

With that, she led Nathaniel out of the gym. Joe and David swapped glances. They were probably thinking there was more to Samantha's decision than met the eye.

Damont draped his arms around Joe and David. "Well," he said with a snicker, "this is an interesting development now, isn't it?"

Wishbone watched Samantha and Nathaniel disappear from view. "Yeah," he said, "very interesting."

Without Samantha, Joe's team just wasn't the same. They looked out of kilter the rest of the game, fumbling passes and missing shots. In fact, they were lucky to come away with a 2–2 tie.

Wishbone didn't see Samantha for almost a week after the game at the gym. In his opinion, that was too bad. Wishbone liked Sam. He liked the way she always found good things to say about people—even Damont. That was a pretty hard thing to do sometimes.

Samantha also loved good books. That was a quality Wishbone admired in her. He liked good books, too, though he probably preferred the classics more than she did.

Mostly, Wishbone appreciated Samantha because she was a good friend—not only to Joe and David, but to him as well. When Joe confided in Sam, he never had to worry. Sam could keep a secret almost as well as Wishbone could.

Then, six days after Samantha left the gym with Nathaniel, Wishbone was taking a walk with Joe in Jackson Park. It was a sunny day, perfect for playing all kinds of great games.

"What do you say?" Wishbone said, looking up at Joe. "You and me and a gnarled, old stick? A little game of fetch?"

It sounded like a great plan to Wishbone. Unfortunately, Joe wasn't very good company just then. He seemed distracted by something—and the terrier could guess what it was.

Samantha, of course. She and David were Joe's best friends, weren't they? After all this time, Joe had to be missing Sam in a big way.

No matter what the reason was, Wishbone didn't like to see his best buddy, Joe, so glum. He looked around for something he could use to cheer Joe up. After a moment or two, his gaze fixed on something gleaming through the branches of a tree.

"Of course," Wishbone said. "Why didn't I think of that before?"

Turning around, he caught hold of Joe's pants leg in his teeth and tugged in a particular direction. Joe looked at Wishbone as if he'd gone crazy.

"What's the matter with you!" Joe exclaimed.

"The problem is, what's the matter with *you,*" Wishbone said. "But rest assured, we're going to take care of that pretty darned quick."

Letting go of Joe, Wishbone took off in the direction of the gleam he had seen. He scooted between a couple of tall trees and leaped over a big, twisted root. Just as Wishbone had expected, Joe followed him at a jog.

"I trained him well," Wishbone said.

He continued to scamper through the woods, careful not to get too far ahead of Joe. Before long, they reached the destination Wishbone had in mind.

They were standing by a little beach beside the

park's big, blue duck pond. None of the ducks happened to be around at the moment. The gleam, of course, had been nothing more than sunlight striking the smooth surface of the water.

Wishbone looked around for a moment and found a flat rock a few inches across. Picking it up in his mouth, he offered it to Joe. The boy tilted his head in a puzzled look. Then he took the rock from Wishbone.

"You want me to skim it?" Joe asked.

"I sure do," Wishbone said. "Then, when you're done, we'll skim some more. If we skim enough stones, I'll bet you'll forget that funk you're in." He looked up at Joe. "At least, I hope so."

Joe looked at the flat rock, then at Wishbone, then at the rock again. He shrugged. Then he positioned the rock in his hand so its edge rested against his forefinger. He pulled his arm back and let it fly, flicking his wrist at just the right moment.

The rock hit the surface of the glittering pond. It

skipped a few feet, hit again, skipped again, hit again, then skipped again. It made five hops in all before it finally sank into the water.

"'Atta boy!" Wishbone said excitedly. "Now we're talking!"

Joe smiled at him. It wasn't a big smile, but it was a start. Looking around, he found another rock and cradled it against his finger. Then he threw it the same way he had thrown the first one.

This time, he got six skips out of the deal. Joe chuckled.

"Yes!" Wishbone exclaimed. "A chuckle. That's real progress. Before you know it, the kid will be grinning from ear to ear."

As Joe reached for another rock, something caught his eye. There was something on the other side of the duck pond. Wishbone followed Joe's gaze to see what the boy found so interesting.

It was Samantha, walking along a tree-shaded path. She wasn't alone. Nathaniel was with her.

The two of them were pushing their bikes side by side, talking and laughing. They were so focused on their conversation that they didn't even notice Joe or Wishbone.

The terrier glanced at his pal. "Joe, there's Samantha," he said. "Maybe she wants to skim some rocks, too."

Joe didn't seem eager to find out. With a sigh, he

stuck his hands in his pockets and tramped off, away from Sam.

"Wait," said Wishbone. "Where are you going?"

Joe disappeared into the woods. Wishbone hesitated for a moment, then followed sadly.

A while later, in Joe's kitchen, Wishbone lay on the floor, his head resting on his paws. Joe and David were slumped at the table, grim faces all around.

"Are we having fun yet?" Wishbone wondered.

This wasn't exactly his day. After seeing Samantha and Nathaniel at the pond in Jackson Park, Joe hadn't wanted to do anything—except mope around in the house.

Then David had come over, and Wishbone had gotten his hopes up for having some fun. He wagged his tail with anticipation, thinking about the boys riding their bikes with a certain four-legged scout blazing a trail in front of them. He imagined them finding adventures under every rock and behind every tree.

But as it turned out, David wasn't in an adventurous mood, either. He was perfectly content to mope around with Joe—especially after Joe told him who he'd seen at Jackson Park. The situation was enough to make even the most patient terrier lose his mind.

Suddenly, the door opened and someone said, "Hi, guys!"

Wishbone turned his head—not that it was the least bit necessary. His keen sense of hearing had already identified the voice and started his tail wagging with anticipation.

It was Ellen, Joe's mom. She was a tall, slender, dark-haired woman. Ellen bustled into the house with a bunch of books in her arms and her handbag dangling from her wrist. She was smiling a big smile, obviously glad to see the kids—and Wishbone, of course—after a long day at work.

Wishbone liked Ellen a lot. But then, what was there not to like? She was the ideal mom, always ready with a kind word or a tasty ginger snap or a welcome scratch behind the ears.

Sure, she had a pretty demanding job as a librarian. She also dreamed of becoming a writer someday. But no matter what life threw at her, Ellen always made sure Joe and his friends came first.

"Together," Wishbone said proudly, "Ellen and I do a darned good job of raising Joe, even if I do say so myself."

Ellen deposited her books on a counter. Then she whipped open her handbag and pulled out her keys. Right about then, she noticed nobody was responding to her. Joe and David were just sitting there, frowning.

"Guys?" she said.

Still no answer. Just a lot of long faces.

"Hello," she said. "Earth to Joe, Earth to David."

Joe looked up at her. "Hi, Mom," he said. But that was all.

"Hi," David added. Not a lot of enthusiasm there, either.

Ellen grunted softly. This wasn't the usual state of affairs. Normally, the boys were as glad to see her as she was to see them.

She studied Joe, then David, and finally Wishbone. "Okay," she said at last. "What's wrong?"

"Don't look at me," Wishbone said. "I'm just an innocent bystander."

Joe shrugged. "It's nothing."

Ellen tilted her head to the side. "Are you sure about that?"

Joe sighed. "I saw Samantha at the park a little while ago."

"And?" said his mom.

"She was with Nathaniel," he added.

"Nathaniel?" Ellen echoed.

David nodded. "Nathaniel Bo-be-lesky!"

"You don't know him," Joe explained to Ellen.

"I see," said his mom. "But . . . what seems to be the problem?"

"Sam's hanging out with him instead of with us," David replied.

"We haven't heard from her in five days," Joe chimed in.

"Six," David said, correcting him.

"Six and a half," Wishbone added, "but who's counting?"

Ellen looked thoughtful for a moment. "Well," she concluded, "maybe Samantha likes Nathaniel."

Joe darted a look at her. "What do you mean?"

"You know," Ellen said. "Like a boyfriend."

Joe and David looked as if they'd swallowed some meat that had gone bad a week ago. *Make that two weeks,* Wishbone thought.

"Boyfriend?" Joe choked. "Nathaniel?"

"No way!" David exclaimed.

No doubt, Ellen could see her idea hadn't cheered the boys up. She tried another smile instead.

"Listen," she told them, "it's just a thought. I'm probably wrong. In any case, I'm sure this problem with Samantha will clear itself up. I'm sure it's just a misunderstanding."

Joe nodded. "Uh-huh."

"Anyway," said Ellen, "I've got some errands to take care of. But we can talk about this some more later on. Okay?"

"Okay," Joe agreed, but without much gusto.

"See you later," his mom said.

Then she kissed Joe good-bye and hurried out to do her errands. As the door closed behind her, Joe and David turned to each other.

"He's not her boyfriend," David insisted.

"Definitely not," Joe confirmed. Then he seemed to waver a little. "But you've got to admit, she's never ever acted like this before."

David frowned, propped his elbows on the table, and sandwiched his head between his hands. "Sam said she was just going to teach him how to skate."

Joe sighed and leaned back in his chair. "That's what she *said.*"

Wishbone stood up. "Boy," he said, glancing at Joe and then David, "these two are really in a bad mood. Somebody had better get to the bottom of this little mystery—and I know just the dog to do it."

Chapter Seven

Leaving the kitchen, Wishbone headed out the back door and sniffed the air. He smelled lots of things.

One of the neighbors was cooking a pot roast—and using a little too much pepper, as far as Wishbone was concerned. Next door, Wanda Gilmore had planted a whole new batch of flowers, mostly lilies and mums. A third neighbor was using a new brand of aftershave.

None of that, however, told Wishbone where Sam and Nathaniel were. Until he found them, there was no way he would find out why they were spending so much time together.

"All right," he said, gathering his wits like any great detective. "Now to track down a couple of missing persons . . ."

It was possible that Sam and Nathaniel were still in the park—possible, but unlikely. After all, Wishbone and Joe had spotted them there a couple of hours ago. By now, they were probably somewhere else.

But where?

The terrier turned in the direction of the street and sauntered down the driveway. On the way, he reviewed his options.

He'd already tried Option One, which was his trusty nose. That hadn't turned up the kind of information he was looking for. Option Two was to send an all-points bulletin to his canine friends in the neighborhood. They had served him well on other occasions—but that method was a last resort.

Besides, Wishbone had a hunch. If Samantha and Nathaniel were spending a lot of time together, they were bound to stop off sometimes at her house . . . or his. If they'd been at either of those places, Wishbone could pick up their scent there and follow it to their current location.

"Anyway," he said, "it's worth a try."

Samantha's house wasn't very far away. Wishbone figured that would be the place to check out first.

With his destination in mind, he took off down the street as fast as his legs would carry him. And that was plenty fast. When Wishbone got going, there wasn't a terrier in the world who could keep up with him.

Resisting the urge to nose around Wanda's newly

replanted garden, Wishbone passed house after house. Finally, Samantha's home stood there in front of him. It was a white-brick building with black trim, as neat and well kept as any other house on the block.

Suddenly, something caught his eye . . . er, nose. In other words, he sniffed something. It was something familiar, too. Slamming on the brakes, Wishbone took a quick look around.

Sure enough, there were Samantha and Nathaniel, dressed in roller-blade gear, skating along on the sidewalk. And unless Wishbone missed his guess, they were headed for Sam's house.

Wishbone wagged his tail happily. "Gosh," he said, "I just love it when I'm right."

Without a moment's hesitation, he concealed himself in some bushes. Then he watched the kids make their way up the block and turn into Samantha's driveway. Only after they had passed him did he leave his hiding place and scamper after them.

After all, he still had a mystery on his hands. Sure, Samantha and Nathaniel were skating *now*—but they hadn't been skating in the park. As far as he was concerned, the jury was still out on the subject of why they were spending so much time together.

Was it to make Nathaniel a better roller hockey player, as Samantha had announced a week earlier? Or was there more to it than that? Wishbone was determined to find out.

As Samantha and Nathaniel tromped into the kitchen, Wishbone estimated the amount of time he had before the door swung shut. There wouldn't be a whole lot of it, he decided.

Another dog wouldn't have had a chance. But Wishbone wasn't just any dog. Putting on a burst of speed, he made for the open doorway as fast as his legs could carry him.

Sure enough, as Sam and Nathaniel let the door swing closed behind them, a speedy white terrier with brown spots scooted in on their heels. Wishbone was quiet enough not to attract their attention. After all, he thought, he might have an opportunity to overhear some clues.

Clunking across the kitchen floor in her roller

blades, Samantha called upstairs. "Hi, Dad," she said. "It's me and Nathaniel."

Sam's father was a likable fellow named Walter. He and Joe's father, Steve, had been friends before Joe's father died.

Walter called back to Samantha from upstairs. He had a deep but friendly voice. "Hi-ya, kiddo. How's it going, Nathaniel?"

"Pretty good, Mr. Kepler."

Sam's father didn't seem the least bit surprised that Nathaniel was there. Wishbone filed that fact away for future reference. Then Nathaniel happened to glance his way, and his cover was blown.

"Look," he said. "It's Wishbone."

Seeing that the jig was up, Wishbone sat down on the kitchen floor in front of Samantha. "Hi," he said. "I just happened to be in the neighborhood, so I thought I'd drop in."

Samantha looked down at him. "Wishbone!" she exclaimed. "But . . . what are you doing here?"

"Oh, don't mind me," he said. "You kids have fun. I'll just sit here in the corner."

Normally, sitting in the corner wasn't Wishbone's style. But a great detective had to blend in with his surroundings sometimes.

"Isn't that Joe's dog?" Nathaniel asked.

"Wishbone is *everyone's* dog," Sam replied. She winked at Nathaniel. "He just sleeps at Joe's house."

Nathaniel chuckled. "I get it."

Samantha closed the door—no doubt to keep any unwanted animals from wandering in. Wishbone knew what a nuisance that could be. Then she and Nathaniel began peeling off their sweaty hockey gear. When they were done, the boy collapsed on a nearby chair.

"I'm pooped," he said.

"You can't be *that* pooped," Samantha said with a smile.

"I am," Nathaniel insisted. "I'm not used to doing so much in one day. Riding bikes in the morning, skating in the afternoon . . ."

". . . builds up your sense of balance," Sam said, finishing the sentence for him. She shrugged. "At least, it should."

"Except in my case," the boy replied. He shook his head sadly. "I've tried, Sam. I really have. But I don't think I'll ever get the hang of it."

"Oh, come on," Samantha said, brightening. "You're making good progress."

"Progress?" Wishbone repeated.

His ears perked up. Clues and more clues. He sifted them through his steel-trap mind.

Nathaniel shot Samantha a skeptical look. "I'm not sure I'd call falling down every other time I skate 'good progress.'"

Every other time he . . . skates? Wishbone thought.

He snorted in disappointment. It appeared that Samantha really *was* teaching Nathaniel to skate, exactly the way she had said she would. But it seemed that she had resorted to some odd methods along the way. Also, no one had expected them to keep at it for so long.

But then, Nathaniel had obviously needed a lot of work. If his comments now were any indication, he still did.

"Relax," Sam advised her pupil. "We've got all the time in the world. Rome wasn't built in a day, you know."

"Neither was Notre Dame cathedral," Wishbone said.

Once again, he began to daydream about the great stone church and its unsightly bell ringer, Quasimodo. . . .

Chapter Eight

Quasimodo's punishment in the square was finally over and done with. He dragged himself up the stone stairs leading to the cathedral. He was so tired his belly grazed the steps. At last, he entered Notre Dame.

It was a big, echoing place with towering ceilings and row after row of wooden pews. Almost everyone in Paris came to worship at the great cathedral at one time or another. Large, multicolored stained-glass windows let in rays of bright light. Candles stood in clusters, breaking up the shadowy darkness in the corners of the huge church.

Notre Dame had a lot of tiny rooms and closets and crannies as well. There were so many, in fact, it was difficult to keep track of them all. Even the hunchback, who had lived in the cathedral all his life, was often delighted to discover a nook he'd never seen before.

During mass, the church was full of organ music and the voices of the priests. Most of the time, however, it was wonderfully quiet—the way it was right now.

Crossing the central space to a door on the far side, Quasimodo found another set of stone stairs. These ran alongside a wall of the cathedral. The winding staircase turned and twisted until it reached the bell tower.

The hunchback ascended the steps as best he could. He drew strength from the idea that he could rest when he was finished climbing. Finally, he reached his destination—the place where he lived alongside the great bells at the top of Notre Dame.

"Home, sweet home," he said.

Needless to say, he was glad to be back. The coolness of the evening air felt really good to him after the punishing heat of the day. He even got to see a full moon—his absolute favorite kind.

The hunchback was just about to go to sleep, exhausted from his terrible ordeal, when he heard sounds below in the square. He got up on all four legs to investigate. It seemed another crowd had gathered at the foot of the cathedral. This time, however, it wasn't to crown a King of Fools, or to witness the humiliation of a poor, innocent bell ringer.

No, this crowd was a rather quiet one. In fact, the only sound that drifted up to Quasimodo from the square below was the tinkling of little bells—the kind one might hear coming from a tambourine. He had a feeling he knew who might be playing it.

Leaning over the little wall that encircled his tower, the hunchback took a closer look at what was going on below. He saw a dark, slender figure weaving her way among the others. Her hair flowed behind her like a banner in the wind. Instantly, Quasimodo's heart leaped in his chest.

It was Esmeralda, all right!

She spun and dipped and swept from one place to another. She was caught up in the rhythms she was creating with her tambourine. No one threw gold coins at her feet. After all, this wasn't the tavern, and these people probably didn't have any money to spare. But Esmeralda didn't seem to care.

As the Gypsy girl danced, the bell ringer saw her in a new light. He knew now that she wasn't only beautiful and graceful. She was also, quite likely, the kindest person in all of Paris. She alone had given him water when everyone else had ignored his suffering and called him hurtful names.

Quasimodo's tail wagged when he thought of Esmeralda. He was happy to know she was on his side. He wished only good things would happen to her, now and always.

He wondered if there was a chance he and Esmeralda might become friends someday—the kind who went on picnics and gave each other presents on their birthdays. Sighing, the bell ringer shook his head at his foolishness.

"You're a hunchback," he told himself. "No one in the world is more feared and disliked. What could a beauty like Esmeralda see in a fellow like you?"

Then he remembered what she had done for him that afternoon. He recalled how brave she had been. He wondered if Esmeralda would have taken that big a chance to help someone if she didn't have at least a *little* affection for that someone.

Suddenly, Quasimodo's ears perked up. He heard another sound. It was the loud clipclop of horses' hooves on the cobblestones of the square. Venturing out onto one of the gargoyles and craning his neck a bit, he saw a battalion of city guards ride up to the crowd.

"Uh-oh," he said. "Here comes trouble."

One of the riders was Phoebus de Chateaupers, the captain of the guards himself. The bell ringer was afraid for Esmeralda. Suddenly, he was certain that she had broken some law and was going to be taken away to jail. Paris had so *many* laws, it was hard to keep track of all of them.

Quasimodo's fear for Esmeralda turned out to be unnecessary. Captain Phoebus, a tall and handsome man, didn't order the Gypsy girl to be arrested. He simply got off his horse and turned its reins over to

one of his fellow guardsmen. Then the captain took Esmeralda aside by her elbow.

The Gypsy girl didn't seem afraid of Phoebus, either. She went with him willingly.

It was difficult for Quasimodo to hear what they were saying. In fact, it would have been difficult for anyone to hear what they were saying, since Phoebus appeared to be whispering into the Gypsy's ear.

Then, with a flourish of his cape, the captain returned to his horse and got back on. As Esmeralda looked on, Phoebus rode away.

For a moment, she just stood there, her head cocked to one side, as if in a trance. Then Esmeralda raised her hand to her mouth and blew the departing Phoebus a kiss.

At least that was how it seemed to Quasimodo. And as imperfect as his hearing was, he had the best eyesight in all of Paris. If he thought he saw something, he was almost always right.

That meant that Esmeralda was . . . in love with Phoebus. And if she was in love with Phoebus . . . she couldn't also be in love with Quasimodo, now, could she? The bell ringer hung his head, heartbroken. His tail drooped.

His friend the cathedral seemed to feel his disappointment. It seemed to say, "Go to sleep, Quasimodo. Forget the affairs of men and women. You belong here in my bell tower, where you are protected from the world's pain."

The hunchback took a last look at Esmeralda. Then he came down off the gargoyle and curled up on the hard, stone floor. It was a long time before he was able to go to sleep.

In the morning, the hunchback awoke, refreshed. A pleasant breeze ruffled his fur. A bright, new sun was rising in the east. It was hard for him to feel bad about anything—especially the lovely Esmeralda.

"If she's happy," he said, "I'm happy for her. It would be selfish of me to think otherwise."

Soon, the pigeons came and landed on Quasimodo's stony friends, the gargoyles, who decorated every corner of the cathedral's tower. He liked the gargoyles. They wore funny expressions that cheered the bell ringer when he was glum.

Actually, gargoyles weren't just decorations. They served a useful function as water spouts. Sticking out from the roof of the cathedral, they threw rainwater clear off the building so it didn't get into cracks and crevices and cause damage.

It was a good thing, too. The hunchback wouldn't have liked living in the tower if it was always wet there.

Digging into his store of bread crumbs, Quasimodo took a bunch of them in his mouth and laid them out on the stone. The pigeons flitted over from their perches on the gargoyles and landed around him. Knowing him as they did, they didn't shy away or peck at him. They simply ate their fill and then moved on.

Soon, it would be time for morning mass. The hunchback would have to ring the bells to call everyone to prayer. For now, though, it was quiet and peaceful in his tower, and he enjoyed the calm while he could.

Unfortunately, it wouldn't remain quiet and peaceful for long.

As Quasimodo raised his snout and sniffed the air, smelling the slow, steady river that surrounded the cathedral and enjoying the company of the pigeons, he saw someone come up the steps that led to his bell tower. His visitor was dressed in fine velvet robes.

It was Dom Frollo, of course. No one else ever bothered to go up there to speak with "that crazy hunchback."

As Quasimodo took a closer look, he saw that Dom Frollo's garments were soiled with mud. That seemed rather strange to the bell ringer. After all, his master was always dressed so neatly.

That wasn't the only thing that seemed strange about Dom Frollo. He had that sweaty, faraway look on his face that Quasimodo had seen the other night in the tavern—a look of wanting but not having.

"Something terrible has happened," Dom Frollo said.

"Come on," Quasimodo replied, wagging his tail for effect. "Cheer up. Things can't be so bad. At least you don't have to walk around with a hunch on your back, the way I do."

"I have a burden that is even heavier than your hunch," his master snarled at him. He held his hands out in front of him and his eyes widened, as if he were looking at something frightening. "There is blood on my hands."

"Yuck and double-yuck," the bell ringer said. He jumped back a step and landed on his paws. "Stay right there, boss. I'll get you a rag, okay?"

"No!" Dom Frollo cried out. He sounded as if he were in pain. "Not *my* blood, you idiot!" He held his hands right up to his face. "It is the blood of Phoebus, captain of the city guards."

"Phoebus?" Quasimodo repeated.

The hunchback didn't understand. Why would Phoebus's blood be on his master's hands? And why was Dom Frollo so upset about it?

"Need I spell it out?" his master asked. "I have killed Captain Phoebus," he moaned loudly.

Quasimodo swallowed hard. "Killed him? You mean . . . you really *killed* him?"

"Yes," Dom Frollo hissed. "I, the most respected man in all of Paris, have committed the most evil crime of all. Murder! Do you hear me? Cold-blooded murder!"

The hunchback couldn't believe it. No wonder his master was so upset. "What happened?" he asked softly.

His master's face twisted as he remembered. "I heard a rumor," said Dom Frollo, "a rumor that Esmeralda had fallen in love with the handsome Phoebus. The very thought burned in my jealous heart like poison."

Quasimodo remembered what he had seen in the square the night before. It seemed what his master had heard was more than a rumor.

"Unable to believe my ears," Frollo went on, "I went to the Gypsies' camp late at night. Sure enough, I saw Esmeralda and Phoebus sitting by themselves in the moonlight."

"There is no crime in that," Quasimodo commented.

Dom Frollo eyed him. "You think not? It was *I* she should have been sitting with. It was *I* she should have loved."

"Er . . . right," the hunchback replied. "Whatever you say, boss."

Dom Frollo's eyes glazed over. "My blood boiled at the sight of them. I couldn't tolerate the pain any longer. So I took out the dagger I'd brought along under my robes—"

Quasimodo gulped. "You brought a *dagger*?"

His master nodded, his eyes narrowing. "And I *used* it."

A chill ran all through the bell ringer's bones. "That's horrible," he said, lowering his face to the ground and covering it with his paws.

It was worse than horrible. It was murder, just as his master had said.

"Then, realizing what I had done," said Dom Frollo, "I became afraid that someone had witnessed my crime. In a fit of panic, I dropped the dagger and ran for all I was worth."

"And . . . ?" the hunchback prodded, eager to hear the rest of the story.

"I escaped into the woods," his master told him. He lowered his eyes. "But Esmeralda was not so fortunate. She was too scared to run. When Phoebus's men came looking for him, she was still sitting by his side—holding the bloody dagger in her innocent hands."

"Ohmigosh!" Quasimodo said, leaping to his feet. "Don't tell me they think *Esmeralda* killed the captain!"

Dom Frollo scowled. "They think Esmeralda killed the captain."

"I asked you *not* to tell me that," the bell ringer groaned.

He knew the punishment for attacking one of the city guards. It was execution on the gallows. In other words . . . death!

Dom Frollo shook his head sadly. "What kind of man am I, to let an innocent girl be punished in my place?"

"Not a very nice one," Quasimodo noted. "Wait a minute. . . . You can still confess and let Esmeralda off the hook. You can tell the judge the truth about what you did."

His master looked at him. "Tell the truth? But then . . . *I* would end up on the gallows, wouldn't I?"

"Well," said the hunchback, "yes, that's the way it usually works. If you commit a crime, you get punished for it."

Dom Frollo turned pale. "No. I can't confess." He swallowed hard. "No matter what, I can't face that fate."

"But it's all right for *Esmeralda* to be hanged in your place?" Quasimodo asked. "Even though she didn't *do* anything?"

It didn't seem fair. The hunchback didn't like being a snitch, but he would have to tell someone the truth about this crime. Otherwise, the Gypsy would pay the price for what Dom Frollo had done.

"I know what you're thinking," his master told him. "You're going to go to the judge and tell him the truth." He snickered. "But who's going to believe you, Quasimodo? Who's going to believe your word over mine?"

Dom Frollo had a point there, the bell ringer admitted. His master was one of the most prominent men in Paris. Quasimodo, on the other hand, was little more than a curiosity to most people.

Still, Quasimodo just couldn't let poor Esmeralda take the blame for his cowardly master. He had to do something.

But . . . what?

Chapter Nine

Suddenly, Wishbone realized that he had been daydreaming again. He was in Samantha's kitchen all by himself.

Where has everyone gone? he thought.

Then he heard voices coming from the living room. Immediately, he recognized them as Sam's and Nathaniel's. Shaking off the cobwebs of his dream, Wishbone began to track down his prey. . . .

That was, until he saw the skateboard sitting in the corner. Samantha's skateboard. The yellow-and-black one. It was just sitting there, looking innocent as could be.

"Hello," Wishbone said. "You again. The thing with the wheels."

It didn't answer, of course. It just glinted in the sunlight coming through the window.

Wishbone felt an urge to investigate the skateboard further. However, he was still on the case. A professional didn't take time to loiter—even if he felt he had already solved his mystery.

So he left the skateboard behind and padded into the living room. That was where he found Nathaniel slumped in a big, overstuffed easy chair. Samantha was standing in front of him with her arms folded across her chest.

As the terrier picked a spot on the hardwood floor and lay down, he heard Nathaniel sigh. "All I want to do," said the boy, "is . . . I don't know . . . just sort of break the ice with . . . you know . . ."

"With *who?"* Wishbone asked.

He perked up his ears. This could be valuable information.

"The guys?" Samantha said.

Nathaniel nodded. "The guys."

Wishbone snuffled. This was a roller-skating thing, all right. There was no doubt about it.

"Cheer up," Sam assured him. "It'll happen."

"How?" Nathaniel asked.

Samantha pondered the question for what seemed like a long time. All her thinking didn't seem to be getting her anywhere. "I'm not sure exactly," she confessed, "but we'll think of something."

Wishbone eyed their feet from his vantage point on the floor. To his trained eyes—and ears and nose—everything seemed kosher. Despite Joe's fears, there was no indication that these two kids were anything but friends.

"Do you want some water?" Samantha offered.

"Thanks," Nathaniel told her. "I could use some."

Sam went back into the kitchen. While she was gone, Nathaniel picked up a framed photo of her dad from the wooden end table. The boy studied it for a moment, then shook his head.

"It must be nice," he said, speaking loudly enough for Sam to hear him in the next room.

"What must be nice?" Samantha asked.

"Having a dad around," Nathaniel explained. "You know, someone to teach you how to play basketball and skate and stuff. I haven't seen my father since I was seven."

Samantha came back into the living room with a glass of water in her hand. "Here you go," she said.

He nodded. "Thanks a lot."

Taking the glass from her, Nathaniel stared into it sadly. He didn't say anything else for a while.

"Are you okay?" Sam asked him.

"I guess," he said. He looked up at her. "You know, when my folks split up, every night I used to wish they would . . . you know . . . get back together. But lately . . ." He shrugged. "I don't know. I mean, they're happier now, so that's good. Right?"

It seemed as if Nathaniel was doing a good job of trying to convince himself. But the tone of his voice told Wishbone that the boy still missed his father very much.

"Right," Samantha said. "I mean . . . I guess so. I still think about the way it was before *my* parents got a divorce."

Her eyes drifted to a glass figurine on the end table—a transparent unicorn with a golden horn. It was a fragile-looking thing, gleaming there in the afternoon light. She picked it up.

"My parents gave me this on my birthday," Samantha said. "The one before they decided to split up."

She and Nathaniel stared at the figurine.

"I keep it," she went on, "because it reminds me that despite everything, we still had some good times together."

Nathaniel smiled. Wishbone thought he knew why, too. The boy was thinking he wasn't the only youngster with divorced parents.

It was kind of a touching scene. But Wishbone had no reason to stick around any longer. He had places to go and people to see.

"Later, *amigos,*" he said.

Getting up, Wishbone made his way back into the kitchen, intending to nudge the door open with his nose and return to headquarters—in other words, his and Joe's house. But before he reached the door, he noticed Samantha's skateboard again, sitting there in the sunlight.

Approaching the thing, Wishbone sniffed it again. Then he tilted his head and looked at it from another angle.

"You're kind of helpless," he said, "without someone to push you around. Aren't you?"

Again, the skateboard didn't respond. Not that Wishbone had expected it to. It sat patiently, waiting for someone to take it for a ride.

"You know," he said, pushing it gently with his nose, "it *is* kind of an interesting unit. Not that I'd want to wear a permanent set of wheels or anything, but still . . . interesting."

Wishbone considered the possibilities. After all, no one was using the skateboard at the moment, and he had to admit that he was kind of curious about it. He'd never ridden a thing with wheels before—except the family car, but that didn't count.

"Okay," he said, "just one quick ride." He lifted his muzzle, striking a noble pose. "In the name of science, of course."

Wishbone went to the back end of the skateboard and gave it a hard shove with his nose, rolling it forward. It moved pretty quickly. With a few quick steps, he hopped on.

The skateboard zipped across the kitchen like the wind. All Wishbone had to do was sit there, enjoying the ride.

"Wheeee!" he said. "This isn't half bad!"

He found himself barreling from the kitchen into the little entry hall by the front door, and from there into the living room. When Wishbone's wheels hit the living room's wooden floor, the ride got a little rougher—but not so rough that he had to leap off.

This was fun. In fact, it was a lot more fun than he had ever imagined.

As Wishbone whisked past Samantha, who was still holding the delicate, glass unicorn, she looked at him as if he'd grown another tail. Her eyes were big and wide. Obviously, the sight of a dog riding a skateboard had taken her completely by surprise.

"Wishbone!" she exclaimed.

Uh-oh, Wishbone thought. *Maybe this would be a good time to stop.* He looked for the skateboard's brakes.

Unfortunately, there weren't any.

Hey, he thought, *how do you stop this thing?*

As surprised as Samantha, and maybe even more so, Nathaniel bolted up from his chair. In the process, he knocked the unicorn out of Samantha's hand, sending it flying high in the air.

The figurine glinted in a beam of light as it flipped head over hooves. To Wishbone, the delicate glass object looked more beautiful than ever—and more fragile, too.

Samantha was horrified. "No!" she cried out.

"Double no!" Wishbone said, knowing what the glass unicorn meant to her. If it broke . . .

He didn't even want to think about it. Anyway, it wasn't the time for thinking. It was the time for *action.*

Bunching his leg muscles, Wishbone leaped off the skateboard as far and as fast as he could. He soon realized, however, that he was too far away to save Samantha's treasured unicorn. He watched helplessly as it reached its high point and then began to fall. It was headed straight for destruction on the hard living room floor.

Then Wishbone saw that he wasn't the only one trying to save the figurine. Nathaniel was diving for it, too.

The boy's body was stretched out as far as it would go. At the very last possible second, he reached for the unicorn . . . and snared it with one hand before it could smash itself on the floor!

Samantha pumped her fist in the air, as overjoyed as Wishbone had ever seen her. "Yes!" she shouted.

"Samantha?" her dad called from upstairs. "Is everything okay down there?"

"Just fine," she answered, with a note of relief in her voice.

Nathaniel was lying on the floor, the unicorn clutched to his chest. Samantha hunkered down beside him.

"Thanks," she said gratefully.

"Er . . . you're welcome," Nathaniel told her, still clutching the figurine. He didn't seem ready to let go of it just yet. It was as if he thought it would shatter if he loosened his grip even a little bit.

Wishbone looked at the boy in a new light. "Wow!" he said. "What a move. I didn't know the kid had it in him."

Samantha gently pried Nathaniel's fingers open and took the figurine from him. He seemed relieved to be rid of it.

As Wishbone watched, Sam put the unicorn back in its place on the end table. It looked safe there, he decided—safe and secure, no matter how many skateboards came whizzing by.

"You know," Wishbone said, "I haven't seen such a timely save since . . . since . . ." He pondered the question for a moment. ". . . Well, since Quasimodo rescued the lovely Esmeralda."

Chapter Ten

Back in the square outside Notre Dame cathedral, where Quasimodo had suffered the day before for a crime he hadn't committed, an even worse injustice was about to take place. But this time, the victim would not be the hunchback.

"Poor Esmeralda," Quasimodo said. He paced around in the cathedral's bell tower and glanced occasionally over the wall. "She's the one in trouble now."

Clutching at some beads she wore around her neck, the Gypsy girl was being led to the gallows that had been built in the square in front of Notre Dame. Surrounding her were a half dozen guards. The crowd that had applauded her dancing the other night was now yelling and taunting her. They were convinced that it was she who had stabbed their beloved Captain Phoebus.

Happily for Phoebus, he had survived his wound

and was recuperating at home. But that didn't do Esmeralda any good. The penalty for attacking a guard was still death, whether the guard himself ended up dying or not.

Dom Frollo, dressed in clean, fine clothes again, stood among the crowd. He looked on with a face as hard as stone—just like his jealous heart. He didn't show the least little sign of the guilt he had described to Quasimodo.

In fact, he was very much at peace with himself. Anyway, it seemed that way on the surface.

The rat! thought the hunchback. The fur around his neck ruffled with anger.

As he watched sadly from the bell tower, he saw Esmeralda's eyes lock on the gallows. A hooded hangman was preparing the rope that would take her life. One of the guards gave her a push onto the stairs.

The Gypsy girl climbed up one step at a time. She showed no sign of fear. Esmeralda gave Quasimodo the impression that she had accepted her fate, no matter how unfair it was.

Then, suddenly, Dom Frollo raced forward and stopped her. He took her hand in his and pleaded with her. But he said everything only in a whisper. That way, no one else could hear what he had to tell Esmeralda.

Of course, Quasimodo didn't have to hear his master's words. He was able to read his lips, even from all the way up in the tower.

"Listen to me," Dom Frollo told Esmeralda. "This is your last chance. I alone can save you."

The Gypsy girl stared at him. She did not have the faintest idea of what he was talking about. "What do you mean?" she asked.

Dom Frollo bit his lip. "It is I for whom you are taking the blame," he admitted. "It was I who stabbed Captain Phoebus the other night, in a fit of jealous rage."

Stunned, Esmeralda pulled her hand back. "You . . . ?" she said. She could hardly believe her ears.

"Yes," Dom Frollo replied. "It was also I who tried to seize you outside the tavern the other night. But don't you see? I can undo all this. I can make everything all right again. One word from your lips is all it will take. Say you will be mine, and your life will be spared."

Esmeralda looked at him. "You stood by as Quasimodo suffered a punishment meant for you . . . and now you would do the same thing to me? You are an evil man, Dom Frollo. Begone this instant . . . or I'll denounce you for the monster you are."

He must have seen the hatred for him expressed in the Gypsy girl's eyes. And seeing it, his heart seemed to turn to stone again.

"Die, then," he told Esmeralda.

Turning away from her, he deprived Esmeralda

of her last hope. The executioner pulled her up the last of the gallows stairs. He wasn't gentle about it, either.

Up there in the tower with his bells, Quasimodo leaned out over the wall on his forepaws and stared down at the terrible, tragic scene below. His heart went out to the doomed Esmeralda.

"My bells won't ring on a sad day like today," he promised. "What a shame. What a terrible ending, after the poor girl showed me such kindness."

The wind seemed especially cold all of a sudden. Quasimodo had a feeling it would stay that way forever. Esmeralda had been a light in his life. Now that light was being put out.

Glancing at one of his gargoyle friends, he asked, "Why was I not made of stone like these?"

After all, if Quasimodo were a statue, he wouldn't have felt Esmeralda's pain. He wouldn't have felt anything. He didn't think he would have minded a gargoyle's feeling of helplessness, since he was so helpless already. . . .

Or *was* he?

Suddenly, Quasimodo snapped to attention. "Wait a minute," he said. "I'm *not* a statue. I'm *not* made of stone. I'm a person. I don't have to sit around here and watch this tragedy take place." He puffed out his furry, white chest. "I can . . . I can do something to prevent it! What's more, I *will!*"

Stirred into action, the hunchback made a daring leap from the bell tower and landed on the ledge below. Then he gathered his four legs and leaped a second time and a third. Each jump brought him closer to Esmeralda and her executioner.

But would he get there in time?

With ever-increasing speed, he made his way down the face of the great cathedral. He threw concern for his safety to the winds. Finally, with one last, soaring bound, Quasimodo came to a skidding, four-pawed landing on the cobblestones . . . just a few feet away from the solemn, gray gallows.

Just like the other day, no one seemed to notice him—at least, not at first. Then, as the executioner lowered the noose over Esmeralda's head, Quasimodo skipped up onto the executioner's platform. Suddenly, the people in the crowd started pointing at him and murmuring.

"Look at that!" someone shouted over the other voices. "It's Quasimodo, the devil!"

"What does he think he's doing up there?" someone else cried out. "He must be loonier than I thought!"

Esmeralda was obviously shocked to see Quasimodo, too. Dom Frollo was just plain angry at the interruption.

"Have no fear!" the bell ringer barked to the innocent Gypsy girl. "Your hero is here!"

With that, Quasimodo chomped down with his teeth on the executioner's ankle. "Drop that rope, stinky! The lady's not for hanging!"

The hangman shrieked and let go of Esmeralda. Instantly, she slipped out of the noose.

"Come on!" the hunchback told her. "We'll be safe in the cathedral!"

With that, he led Esmeralda down the gallows stairs to the ground. But before they could get very far, Dom Frollo blocked their path. His teeth ground together with hatred and frustration as he glared down at Quasimodo.

The bell ringer had never imagined a moment like this, when he and Dom Frollo would be squaring off as enemies. After all, he owed the man his very existence.

But Dom Frollo had only thrown Quasimodo a few scraps when it suited his purposes. He had never treated the hunchback with dignity and respect—not the way Esmeralda had.

Besides, the Gypsy girl's soul was pure and innocent as spring water. Dom Frollo's soul was dark as coal. The people in the square had mockingly called Quasimodo a devil—but the real devil was the man in the velvet robes.

"Stop!" Dom Frollo snapped. He pointed a spindly finger at the bell ringer. "I am your master!"

"Not anymore!" Quasimodo responded.

The hunchback dashed under Dom Frollo's legs, all four of his own legs churning as fast as they could go. Dom Frollo reached down for Quasimodo, but he missed. Losing his balance, he tumbled to the ground and banged his head on the cobblestones.

One of the guards tried to stop Quasimodo, as well. But the hunchback ran circles around the man, making him stagger with dizziness until he fell.

Two other guards ran at Quasimodo from opposite directions. They looked as if they would trap the bell ringer between them. However, he eluded their clutches with a burst of speed, causing them to bang their heads together and collapse in a tangle.

Suddenly, Quasimodo heard a bellow of triumph. Just in time, he turned to see the executioner diving at him, his arms outstretched. Leaping into the air and out of the way, the hunchback saw the executioner land with a jolt on the hard ground. The man's cry of victory quickly turned into a cry of pain.

Quasimodo landed on the man's back. Then, before the executioner could have another chance to grab him, he scooted away.

But the bell ringer hadn't come down to the square just to run the city guards ragged. He had come to rescue the fair Esmeralda.

Finding her in the midst of the confused onlookers, Quasimodo rejoined her. Then he made a ruckus and parted the crowd so the two of them could make their getaway.

"Excuse me," he yelped. "We're coming through. Make way, people. Escape in progress. Make way!"

In front of them stood the cathedral. It had been a place of safety and security for as long as Quasimodo could remember. If he and Esmeralda could make it inside, they would be all right there.

"Come on!" he yipped. "This-a-way!"

As quickly as they could, the hunchback and the Gypsy girl ran up the steps of the cathedral and darted through the huge open doors. Looking back over his shoulder, Quasimodo saw that the city guards weren't far behind. They didn't look at all amused by the chase he had led them on.

"Sanctuary!" he barked at them, seeking safety in the church. "Sanctuary!" Then, just for good measure, he yelled at the top of his lungs: *"Sanctuary!"*

The cry echoed throughout the square, commanding the attention of everyone assembled there. The people stood transfixed, as if they were statues, their mouths and eyes alike opened wide at Quasimodo's boldness.

But the city guards were not impressed. They plunged ahead, hoping to grab the hunchback and the Gypsy girl before they could get away.

Quasimodo put his nose to the cathedral's big, wooden doors. He pushed them closed as quickly as he could. Then he slammed the bolt into place behind the doors—just as the guards were about to pounce on him and Esmeralda. After the hunchback's valiant effort, all was quiet.

However, the silence ended when the guards started banging on the doors, trying their best to get inside.

Chapter Eleven

"Let's go!" barked Quasimodo.

Running as fast as his feet could carry him, he led Esmeralda across the cold, stone floor of the church. They ran past the beams of colored light that streamed in through the stained-glass windows.

"Where are we going?" she asked him.

Passing a bunch of candles, they came to the door where the winding stairs to the bell tower began. "Up here!" he told her, taking the steps two at a time.

The Gypsy girl didn't question the hunchback any further. She just scampered after him, trusting that he knew what he was doing. Quasimodo desperately hoped he had done enough to be worthy of that trust.

After all, he *had* called for "sanctuary."

Sanctuary was an important idea in the Middle Ages. If someone had broken a law, he could claim "sanctuary" by ducking into a church or a royal palace.

He would be safe there. The city guards couldn't hurt him or drag him out against his will.

That was important, because a lot of laws weren't very fair at the time. If not for the protection of sanctuary, a lot of people would have received serious punishments for even the smallest crimes.

It was a nice concept, in theory. *The problem,* Quasimodo thought, as he continued to climb the stone steps, *is that not everyone believes in the idea of sanctuary. Some people have to be* convinced.

By the time Quasimodo reached the top of the steps, he was a little winded. But he still had enough energy to cross the floor of the tower and lean out over the wall that surrounded it.

Down below, the half-dozen city guards were still pounding on the doors of the cathedral, trying to get in. If they did gain entry, the hunchback didn't have any doubt about what they would do. They would find Esmeralda and return her to the executioner so fast it would make her head spin.

Quasimodo was determined not to let them capture her. If necessary, he was prepared to defend her with his life.

"That's a last resort, though," he reminded himself reasonably. "It's very much a last resort."

Exhausted and gasping for air, Esmeralda leaned back against a stone wall and slid to the floor. Brushing aside a lock of her thick, black hair, she gazed at Quasimodo with her dark, mysterious eyes.

"Thank you," she gasped. "You saved my life."

"Not yet," he told her. "The city guards are not being very civilized about this. They still insist on the pleasure of your company."

Quasimodo heard more pounding from downstairs. Those doors wouldn't last forever, he told himself. If he didn't do something—and quickly—the guards would force their way into Notre Dame.

"What to do?" he said. He paced back and forth on his four legs, trying to ignore the endless pounding noises. "What to do, what to do . . ."

Suddenly, he had an idea. After all, it had been a long time since this high part of the cathedral had been repaired. There were a lot of loose stones and pieces of wood lying around, if one knew where to find them.

No one knew this place better than Quasimodo the bell ringer. "Come on!" he said to Esmeralda. "Give me a hand!"

She stared at him, not knowing what he wanted. "With what?" she asked.

By way of an explanation, the hunchback got behind a heavy piece of stonework. He used his nose to nudge it out into the open. However, judging by her expression, Esmeralda still didn't get Quasimodo's point.

"We need to get the drop on our friends down in the square," he explained, "if you know what I mean."

Abruptly, Esmeralda's eyes lit up with understanding. "Yes," she replied, "I believe I do know what you mean."

The pounding on the cathedral doors was getting louder and louder. Quasimodo and Esmeralda could hear it echoing in the church below.

"Hurry!" yelped the hunchback.

Together they found a variety of objects that could serve as weapons. Quasimodo nudged some of them across the floor with his nose. Esmeralda gathered the rest of the stuff in her arms. Together they placed it all on the little wall. When the hunchback thought they had enough, he told his friend to step back.

Taking a deep breath and hoping for the best, Quasimodo used his nose to push a piece of stone over the edge. Then another. And another.

He heard cries from down below. The guards weren't happy at all about the junk falling all around them. Though none of them had been hit yet, the way all that debris cracked on the cobblestones had to make them think twice about coming after Esmeralda.

But that didn't mean it was okay to stop. If the guards saw that, they might get their courage back. No—Quasimodo and Esmeralda had to show that they meant business. They had to dump even more stuff than before.

"Let's pour it on!" the bell ringer barked.

And they did. Between them, they shoved over the wall every piece of stone, every beam of wood, every chunk of building material they could find. It shattered in front of the cathedral like a bunch of very big and strange-looking hailstones.

When Quasimodo and Esmeralda were done, the city guards had retreated to a safe distance on the far side of the cathedral square. If the looks on their faces were any indication, they wouldn't dare go near Notre Dame's doors again—not even if the king himself ordered them to.

"Hah!" cried the bell ringer, his tail wagging even though he was bone-tired. "We did it!"

His heart was bursting with joy and triumph. He leaped at one of the ropes dangling from his beloved bells and caught it in his teeth. Then, his paws churning, he swung back and forth, causing the bell to ring as it had never rung before.

Next, he leaped to the second rope, and got that bell clanging. Finally, he clamped his teeth on the third rope and got that bell going as well.

And why not? he thought. *Isn't this something to celebrate? Isn't this the absolute best thing I've ever done?*

Then Quasimodo saw the way Esmeralda was looking at him. Part of her, it seemed, shared in his gladness. But another part still didn't know what to make of him.

Leaping down from the bell rope, he landed as far away from her as he could. After all, he didn't want to disgust her.

"I know," he said. "I'm pretty scary-looking with this hump and all."

"It's not that," the Gypsy girl replied. "I just . . . I mean . . . I don't understand. Why did you place yourself in danger to save me from hanging on the gallows?"

The hunchback looked at her. The question had caught him by surprise. "Why?" he echoed. "You mean you've forgotten?"

"Forgotten what?" she asked.

He tilted his head, the breeze ruffling his fur. "Forgotten a poor, misshapen wretch, of course. I am the ugly soul to whom you brought relief, when I was sizzling in the square like an egg on a fiery-hot skillet. You gave me a drink of water and a little pity, when no one else down there would. If that kindness you showed has slipped your mind, it surely hasn't slipped mine."

"No," Esmeralda said. "It hasn't slipped my mind at all. But if you'll pardon my saying so, mine was such a small kindness, and yours has been such a great one."

Quasimodo snorted. "I don't think any act of mercy is too unimportant to be rewarded. What you call a small kindness is by far the greatest gift I've ever received."

The Gypsy girl's brow creased as she thought about the hunchback's words. At last, she nodded. "I see."

"So do I," said a voice.

Whirling, Quasimodo saw the tall, sinister form of Dom Frollo. He was standing at the head of the bell ringer's private stairs. His fine clothes were soiled with dirt again. His forehead was bruised and bloody where it had struck the ground.

Dom Frollo didn't look very happy. In fact, he had what the hunchback could only describe as a *murderous* look in his eyes.

"And what I see," the man continued, "are two lawbreakers trying to escape the justice of the French courts. But they won't succeed—at least, not if I can help it."

"How did you get into the cathedral?" Esmeralda wondered.

"My master . . . er, make that *former* master . . . has a secret set of keys to the place," Quasimodo explained. "After all, he's a pretty important man."

Dom Frollo grunted, as if to show he agreed. Then he took a threatening step toward Esmeralda. Gasping, the Gypsy girl backed up against the little wall that surrounded the tower.

"Stay back," she pleaded, glancing nervously at the cobblestoned square below.

"Er . . . let's not be hasty here," the hunchback

suggested to Dom Frollo. "Let's stop and think a minute."

After all, Dom Frollo *had* fed and clothed Quasimodo all his life. If there was a peaceful way to settle this . . .

"I'll bet if we try," the hunchback told Dom Frollo, "we can sit down and talk this all out. Hey, I know—I'll put up a nice pot of tea. And I've got a few old biscuits, I think. Everyone likes biscuits."

"Do what you like," Dom Frollo snapped. "But keep out of my way—if you know what's good for you."

He took another step toward Esmeralda, his eyes narrowed with evil intent. His hands clenched and unclenched, as if they couldn't wait to grab the Gypsy girl by her neck.

"Listen," said Quasimodo, his fur standing up and bristling, "I know you raised me from a pup and all, but I can't let you hurt my friend here—especially since we both know it was *you* who stabbed Captain Phoebus, not *her.*"

Dom Frollo glared at him. "Only the three of us know that. And pretty soon, it will only be two."

Then Dom Frollo turned back to Esmeralda. Without warning, he ran toward her, his arms outstretched. It was clear that he meant to push her over the wall and send her plummeting to her death.

Quasimodo couldn't let that happen. As Dom

Frollo threw himself at the Gypsy girl, the hunchback leaped, pushing off with his hind legs and coming down hard on the man's back.

"Get off me!" Dom Frollo yelled. "Get off, you monstrous, misshapen lump!"

Suddenly, Dom Frollo tripped and went sprawling. His robes fluttered all around him like the wings of some gigantic bird. Pigeons scattered wildly in his path, fluttering wings of their own.

Quasimodo himself tumbled to the floor. He hoped he had stopped Dom Frollo from pushing Esmeralda to her death. But as he came to a sliding halt, he couldn't be sure.

Then he stopped sliding. And in a heart-stopping moment, the hunchback saw clearly the results of his action.

Barely able to keep himself upright, Dom Frollo missed Esmeralda entirely. Suddenly, he himself was flying over the little wall, a roar of terror and panic following him as he vanished from sight.

"Uh-oh," the bell ringer said.

Leaning out over the wall, Quasimodo saw Dom Frollo tumble down the sloping side of the lofty cathedral. The man clawed frantically at the stone with his manicured nails in an attempt to stop his fall. But it was of no use. There was nothing for the man's nails to dig into.

Dom Frollo landed with a bone-crunching jolt on

a hard stone gargoyle. For a moment, it looked as if he might be able to grab hold of the gargoyle and remain there, and in that way save his life.

Then he began to slip again, despite his best efforts. With a blood-curdling scream, Dom Frollo took the long, deadly plunge to the cobblestoned square below.

Quasimodo turned away, unable to look at the rest. "Ouch!" he said, sympathizing. "That's got to hurt."

He hadn't intended to hurt Dom Frollo. His intention was only to keep him from harming the Gypsy girl. But in a way, it wasn't the hunchback who had done him in. It was Dom Frollo's own evil nature.

Quasimodo turned to Esmeralda. She seemed a little shaken, but unharmed. Unexpectedly, she reached out and took the bell ringer in her arms and hugged him to her.

Quasimodo's tail wagged as he basked in her warmth. It would have been all right with him if she had never, ever let him go. But after a while, she gently put him back on the ground.

On all fours again, the hunchback looked up at her, his tail still wagging merrily. "Not that I'm complaining, mind you . . . but what was that for?"

The Gypsy girl smiled and stroked his head. "Quasimodo," she said, "at this moment, you are truly . . . beautiful."

The hunchback didn't know what to say. No one had ever told him anything like that before.

Of course, he had never saved anyone's life before. He had never been a hero. Or maybe, just maybe, he had always been one—and it had taken Esmeralda's friendship and kindness to bring it out of him.

Suddenly, Quasimodo had the strangest feeling that the Gypsy girl wasn't the only one smiling at him. Looking up, he imagined the great cathedral was smiling, too, as if it was proud of its resident bell ringer.

Finally finding some words, Quasimodo turned to Esmeralda again and shrugged. "It wasn't anything any other brave, quick-witted hunchback wouldn't have done."

Chapter Twelve

Wishbone was so busy enjoying the feeling of being petted, it took him a moment to realize it wasn't just happening in his daydream. It was happening in real life.

And it wasn't the lovely Esmeralda stroking his fur. It was the lovely Samantha. But for the life of him, Wishbone couldn't figure out why.

After all, hadn't he scooted around on her skateboard without permission? Hadn't he acted like an irresponsible pup? Hadn't he come within a hair of demolishing her favorite figurine?

Yet there she was, petting him like crazy. "Good boy!" Sam exclaimed. "You did it, Wishbone! You did it!"

Inwardly, Wishbone laughed. "Of course I did. Don't I always?" He looked at her. "Er . . . did what, exactly?"

Samantha grinned. "If you hadn't gotten on my skateboard, we would never have found out the way we're going to help Nathaniel break the ice—with the guys at the gym, I mean."

Wishbone was still kind of confused. "Mmm . . . okay," he said. "Whatever you say."

Nathaniel was sitting on the living room floor with his legs crossed. He seemed dazed.

Sam turned to him. "Do you know what you just did?" she asked.

Nathaniel looked up at her. "I . . . I just . . . I don't know," he said finally. "It was . . . and I saw . . ." He reached out just the way he had before, his fingers closing on an imaginary object. "Then I caught it."

"You sure did," Samantha said. "Let's get to work, Nathaniel."

"Work?" he echoed.

"Work," she confirmed.

Nathaniel looked at Wishbone. Wishbone looked back at him. Neither of them had any idea what Samantha was talking about . . . but Wishbone had a feeling they were going to find out.

The next day, Wishbone was back where it all started. He lounged outside by the gym door and soaked up a little sun. The kids were there, too, gathered inside for another game of blade hockey.

Damont and the players around him were feeling frisky. Joe and David, on the other hand, were sitting in the bleachers with long faces, pretending to inspect their sticks.

Damont skated up to them. "Come on," he said, "what are we waiting for? Let's play already."

Joe shrugged. "I don't feel like it."

"I don't, either," David said.

Damont frowned. "Just because Samantha dumped you doesn't mean you have to cry about it."

Joe lifted his head and stared at Damont. "She didn't dump us," he insisted. There was a definite tone of annoyance in his voice.

"That's right," David joined in.

"No?" Damont replied. "Then where *is* she?"

David shrugged. "How should I know?"

"I thought Samantha was your best friend," Damont pressed.

Neither Joe nor David had an answer for that.

Suddenly, something on the street caught Wishbone's attention. It was something *good.* At least he was sure Joe and David would think so.

"Hey, guys!" he said. "Guys!" Wishbone dashed into the gym, more excited than he'd been in a long, long time. "Have I got good news for you!"

Joe looked at the terrier, his forehead wrinkling.

"What are *you* so excited about, boy? It's not even lunchtime."

"You're not going to believe it," Wishbone said. "Just wait, okay? Here they come."

At that precise moment, Samantha and Nathaniel skated into the gym in full roller-blading gear. Nathaniel was still a bit awkward on his wheels, but not as much as before.

Joe, David, and Damont skated up to meet them. They seemed more curious than anything else.

"Hi, guys," Samantha said with a chuckle. She wore a grin on her face. "Long time, no see."

Joe played it cool, obviously not wanting Sam to know how much he had missed her. "Oh, really?" he replied.

"We hadn't noticed," David added casually, as if he didn't care the least little bit.

Sam stared at them. "Get serious. We've been gone for days."

"Funny," David replied. "It didn't seem like more than a few hours."

"Enough chitchat," Damont announced. "Let's play."

"Great idea," Samantha responded.

Damont was flipping the hockey ball in the air. With a flick of her wrist, Sam reached out and snagged it.

"This will give me a chance to show you the best new hockey player in town," she said.

Damont looked at her. He was obviously not happy at having had the ball snatched away from him.

"The best new hockey player in town?" he jeered. "Who's that, Samantha? You, I suppose?"

Sam shook her head. "No, silly. *Him.*"

She pointed to Nathaniel.

Damont looked at some of the other kids, to see if Sam was playing a joke on him. They shrugged, showing they didn't understand her, either.

"No way," Damont told Samantha.

"Er . . . maybe I should go," Nathaniel suggested.

"No, Nathaniel," Samantha insisted. The way her jaw clenched told Wishbone she meant business. "It's time for you to play."

By then, Joe had had enough. He grabbed Samantha by the elbow and led her away. David followed them.

"What's your problem?" Samantha asked Joe.

"*My* problem?" Joe responded, his eyes opening wide. "*You're* the problem—you and your new buddy, Nathaniel."

"What are you talking about?" she asked.

"All you ever do is hang out with him," Joe said. "I saw you the other day in the park. The two of you are inseparable."

"Listen, I'm just trying to be nice," Samantha explained. She cast a glance at Nathaniel. "The guy needs a friend."

Joe tilted his head to indicate David. "So do we."

Samantha looked at Joe, then at David, then at Joe again. "Oh, come on, you guys. This isn't like some kind of competition. It's not as if he wins and you lose. I mean, you're still my best friends."

David seemed surprised. "We are?"

"Yes," Sam assured him. "Absolutely."

Joe looked a little confused. "Then, you mean you're not Nathaniel's girlfriend or anything?"

Samantha gaped at Joe and David as if they'd accused her of having two heads. "You thought that . . . that I was . . . he and I were . . ." She laughed a deep belly laugh. "You guys!"

The boys were obviously satisfied with their friend's explanation. They smiled at each other.

"Sam's back!" David said.

"It looks that way," Joe agreed happily.

He motioned to Nathaniel, who was standing at the other end of the gym.

"But come on, Sam. About Nathaniel playing . . . you've got to be kidding, right?"

"I'm *not* kidding," Samantha said stubbornly. "He can really play."

Joe made a face. "But he's . . . you know . . . clumsy."

"Appearances can be deceiving," Sam pointed out. With that, she flipped the ball to Joe and skated away.

Joe looked at David for an explanation. David could only shake his head, showing Joe he didn't *have* an explanation.

A few moments later, the game got started. Nathaniel, with all his gear on, wound up standing in the goalie position for Joe's team. He still looked a little wobbly on his skates.

But that was okay—at least, according to Samantha and her plan.

Wishbone was really excited about this game. Even more than the last one, it had a feeling of drama about it, a sense of mighty forces clashing on the field of battle.

To top it off, Nathaniel was involved in a little drama of his own. But in his case, it wasn't the opposing team he was up against. He was struggling with himself—with his own fears and uncertainties.

Wishbone wished he could help Nathaniel win his struggle. But no one could do that except Nathaniel himself.

Hopping up on the first row of bleacher seats, Wishbone watched the kids go through their pre-game warm-ups. They looked as excited as he was. But then, their last game had ended in a tie, and there was something a little unsatisfying about that.

In fact, if the rumors were true, Damont's team had been practicing every other day. Needless to say, they were looking forward to a victory. But

Joe's team was confident, too. After all, they had Samantha back.

Treading up and down the bleacher seats, wagging his tail as he went, Wishbone felt like the announcer at a professional sporting event. "Are you ready to rumble?" he said. Speaking for the kids, he answered his own question: "You bet we are!"

The game was supposed to last for half an hour. Glancing at the clock on the wall, Wishbone saw it was ten minutes after eleven. At eleven-forty, they would know which squad had come out on top.

As if on cue, the two teams met in the middle of the floor. Joe and Damont faced off to see who would get the red ball first. As it happened, Damont won the face-off, slapping the ball to one of his teammates.

"And the battle's on!" Wishbone said. He was so full of enthusiasm that he could barely contain himself.

Chapter Thirteen

The battle was on, all right. And with Damont's team in possession of the ball, it looked as if Nathaniel would be tested right from the start.

As everyone skated toward Nathaniel's end of the floor, he looked a little nervous. Well . . . maybe more than just a little. Maybe a lot.

"Stay cool," Wishbone said, encouraging Nathaniel. "Just stay cool, kid. You can do it."

Damont and Colby passed the ball back and forth as they sped toward the net. David and Sam tried their best to take the ball away, but they were a step too far behind.

The closer Damont and his teammate got, the more jittery Nathaniel seemed to become. Wishbone began to get jittery, too, just watching him.

"I don't know about this," Nathaniel groaned—though, of course, Wishbone was the only one in the gym who heard him.

For a moment, it looked as if Damont would be the one to take the shot. Then, at the last possible second, he passed the ball to Colby, who drew his stick back and unleashed a wicked slapshot.

Wishbone could see Nathaniel stick his glove out and close his eyes. The ball soared through the air, almost too fast even for Wishbone to see. He heard a resounding *thwack*—like a really loud high-five.

Slowly, Nathaniel opened his eyes, looked into his mitt, and discovered the ball inside—in the *mitt,* not the goal net!

"Yes!" he cried out.

Joe's mouth dropped open. He looked at David. Then the two of them stared at Samantha, who just smiled.

Colby was annoyed as he skated over to Damont. "I thought you said this guy was a pushover," he snapped.

"I thought he was," Damont replied, as surprised as anyone.

"Ha-ha!" Wishbone said. "Save number one—the first of many!"

As the game progressed, Wishbone raced up and down the sideline, describing the action to himself play by play.

"Joe gets the rebound and dumps it off to Samantha. Samantha passes it to David. Oh, no—it's stolen by

Damont! But wait—David's stolen it back now! My gosh, what a game!"

That was the way the contest proceeded for a while, back and forth. Neither team could gain the advantage for long.

Finally, Tina got hold of the ball and began weaving through traffic, cheered on by Damont and her other teammates. She got within half a dozen feet of the goal before she pulled her stick back and fired away.

Nathaniel was still in goal for Joe's team. His eyes grew as wide as doggie dishes when the ball sailed in his direction.

"There's the shot . . ." Wishbone said, holding his breath.

This time, Nathaniel tried to block the ball by sliding his skate over. He made it just in time, sending the ball careening back past Tina toward the center of the gym.

"Nathaniel makes another save!" Wishbone rejoiced. "And the hometown fans go wild!"

Collecting the ball on her stick, Samantha started a break in the other direction. She passed the ball up to David, who passed it along to Joe. But as Joe skated for the goal, Samantha was only a couple of strides behind him.

Wishbone jumped up on his hind legs as he realized what they were up to. Right on cue, Damont and Colby came over from the wings to help block the goal. Joe rushed up as fast as he could. He gave everyone on the opposing team the idea that he'd be taking the shot.

Pulling over to the right, Joe took Damont and Colby with him. Then, instead of shooting, he flipped the ball in back of him. Samantha was waiting right there for it with a big smile on her face.

"Oh, no!" shouted the Damonster, realizing how he'd been hoodwinked—and not for the first time. "Oh, no!"

"Oh, yes!" said Wishbone.

Sam pulled her stick back and unleashed a mighty shot. The ball went hurtling toward the goal.

Anthony, a red-haired boy who was on Damont's team, went diving in front of the net to try to deflect the shot. Unfortunately for him, the ball got by him. Even more unfortunately, his dive made it harder for Damont's goalie to see what he was doing.

Before they knew it, the ball had slammed into the back of the net. The score was 1–0 in favor of Joe's team.

To celebrate, Wishbone executed a perfect back flip. "What a move!" he said. "What a shot! What a game!"

Joe and his teammates were excited, too. They met back at midcourt to exchange high-fives and congratulate one another. But none of them was more excited than Nathaniel. Obviously, the kid was a team player.

As the excitement over the goal died down, Nathaniel returned to his net. Colby and David hunkered down for a face-off. Colby got the best of it, slapping the ball to Damont.

Samantha managed to take it away from him as he sped downcourt. Tina squirted ahead of her, though, and somehow took the ball back. Tina passed to Anthony. Anthony passed to Damont.

Suddenly, Damont was leading the charge from one end of the floor to the other. He had a teammate on either side of him, with Joe's team struggling to catch up. Damont grinned as he approached the goal. He knew it was three on one, and the odds were in his favor.

Nathaniel just stood there, looking very much alone. Without any of his teammates around to help him, he really *was* alone.

As Joe had done, Damont waited until the last second. Then he passed the ball crisply to Colby. Winding up, Colby smacked a wicked slapshot at the goal.

Nathaniel was right on it. He reached out with his stick and knocked the ball away.

"What?" blurted Damont.

He must have thought his team had tied the game up for sure. Thanks to Nathaniel, however, Joe's squad still had the lead.

"The kid's a brick wall out there!" Wishbone said.

One of Joe's teammates got the rebound and started for the other end of the floor. The action was getting faster and more furious. Kids were yelling and wheels were clacking and sticks were banging together.

Wishbone glanced at the clock.

It was eleven thirty-five. There were only five minutes to play. Could Joe's team hold the lead? Would Damont's group come storming back to tie . . . or maybe even win the game?

Only time would tell.

Sitting on the edge of his seat, Wishbone watched the ball bounce from stick to stick. It got harder and harder for either side to complete a pass, much less make a run at the other team's goal. Both goalies tried to stay ready, but the action on the floor was too frantic for them to get a clear view of the ball.

The clock read eleven thirty-seven . . . thirty-eight . . . thirty-nine. Time was running out for Damont's teammates. If they were going to do something, they would have to do it quickly.

There was less than a minute left. It looked more and more as if Joe's team would win the struggle. Then Damont intercepted the ball and emerged from the pack. Even more, he was all alone, with a clear path to the net.

Nathaniel was the only obstacle in his way. As Wishbone watched, Nathaniel bent his knees, bracing himself for the shot. He looked as tense as a rubber band stretched to its limit.

Wishbone lowered his belly to the bleacher seat below him and gritted his teeth. "This is it," he said, barely able to look. "The big showdown. The battle of the titans."

Damont drove in on Nathaniel, a look of pure determination on his face. He knew that the outcome of the game depended on what happened next.

"It's Damont and Nathaniel!" Wishbone said. "Nathaniel and Damont! Damont and Nathaniel, for all the marbles!"

Damont flicked the ball back and forth on his stick, eyeing the goal. Nathaniel shifted this way and that. He reacted every time the ball moved from one side to the other.

Finally, with only a few seconds left on the clock, Damont pulled his stick back as high as he could. With a loud grunt, he took his shot.

The rubber ball whizzed through the air so fast that Wishbone could barely see it. As far as he could tell, it was heading for the upper lefthand corner of Nathaniel's net.

"Uh-oh. Tie game," said Wishbone.

For once, the terrier was wrong. Moving even faster than he had in Samantha's living room, Nathaniel threw his glove hand out and snatched the ball from the air.

"Another save!" Wishbone cheered. "I don't believe it! The kid's done it again! He's done it again!"

Damont, who had twisted around to watch what he thought would be a goal, suddenly lost his balance. With a little shuffle of desperation, he fell awkwardly and slid past the net.

"Game over!" Wishbone whooped. He stood up on his hind legs and hopped around. "Joe's team wins! Joe's team wins!"

Grinning, Joe led the charge toward Nathaniel. The goalie just stood there, not knowing what to do. Of course, he didn't have to do anything. Joe and his teammates did it all. They leaped on top of Nathaniel and gave one another high-fives that sounded like thunderclaps.

Joe ruffled Nathaniel's hair as he helped him to his feet. "Hey, Nathaniel, why didn't you tell us *before* that you could do that?"

His hair all messed up, Nathaniel shrugged and smiled at Samantha. "I guess I needed a little help to find out myself."

Damont skated up and grabbed Nathaniel by his shirtfront. He looked angry. Damont didn't like to lose.

"Awright," he said in his bossiest voice, "I get Bobelesky here at goalie next game."

"Oh, no, you don't," Samantha argued. "Joe picked him and you didn't. He's on *our* team."

"That's right," Joe said, agreeing with Sam.

"Yeah," David chimed in. "And like I always say, the team that plays together stays together."

Damont looked from Joe to David to Samantha. Seeing that he wasn't going to get anywhere, the boy made a sound of disgust. Then he let go of Nathaniel's shirt and skated away.

Wishbone was happy for Nathaniel. "Good for him," he said. "He's learned a valuable lesson—everybody's got something to crow about if they look inside themselves. Just like good ol' Quasimodo."

Samantha tossed the red ball high into the air over her shoulder.

Wishbone bunched his muscles. "On the other hand," he said, "there's one thing Nathaniel *didn't* learn."

Taking a flying leap, the terrier snapped at the ball in midair and caught it in his mouth. Then he landed and grinned around the ball, his tail wagging with satisfaction.

Nathaniel laughed with delight and pointed to Wishbone. "Did you see that?" he asked Joe, David, and Samantha.

"I saw it, all right," said Sam. She smiled and clapped her hands. "Bravo, Wishbone. You'll do *anything* to get applause, won't you?"

Wishbone turned his nose up in make-believe distaste. "What would you expect," he said, "from a world-class performer?"

After all, if there was one thing the terrier was good at, it was pleasing a crowd.

About Victor Hugo

Victor-Marie Hugo was perhaps the most famous and successful European poet, dramatist, novelist, and literary critic of the nineteenth century. He was also a great supporter of the idea that any person, no matter how lowly he or she may seem, has the potential for nobility.

Born in February 1802, Hugo was the third son of a prosperous French military officer. He spent much of his childhood living in fancy houses all over Europe and attending the best schools. But his godfather, who had come to live with Hugo's family when the boy was eight, taught him to have a love of freedom and equality and an appreciation of the common man.

When Hugo was fifteen, his talent for writing was confirmed when he won a major French poetry contest. Before long, his books of verse became best-sellers, and the novels that followed them were just as profitable.

By the time he was twenty-eight, Hugo had married, become the father of four children, and was known as a great romantic writer—one of the best in all of Europe. In 1831, he wrote *Notre-Dame de Paris*—the book we know as *The Hunchback of Notre Dame*. After that, his fame as a novelist was assured.

Later in life, as an elected representative in the French government, Hugo argued on behalf of the common people of France. However, for daring to speak out against a would-be dictator named Louis Napoleon, the writer was forced into exile in 1851, and he left his beloved France.

In 1865, residing in England, he wrote the novel *Les Misérables.* It was an attack on those who would abuse the poor and rob them of their dignity. With the election of a new government in France, Hugo later returned to his homeland, where he was embraced by his fellow French citizens with love and respect.

Hugo's eightieth birthday was celebrated in France as a national holiday. A forceful and eloquent voice for the rights of the oppressed and the downtrodden, he died of pneumonia in May 1885.

About *The Hunchback of Notre Dame*

During a visit to the splendid Parisian cathedral of Notre Dame, writer Victor Hugo—already one of the most prominent young authors of his time—noticed a word carved into the stone wall of one of the cathedral's lofty towers.

The word was the Greek term for "fate"—the idea that all things in our lives are determined by Heaven long before we are born. Intrigued and inspired by this curious inscription, Hugo went on to write a novel about the various aspects of man's nature—both good and bad—and told of how difficult it is to escape the fates intended for us.

There are three principal characters in this novel. First is Dom Claude Frollo, who shows the destructive nature of jealousy. The second is the Gypsy girl, Esmeralda, who represents joy and childlike innocence. The third is an ugly, misshapen hunchback named Quasimodo, who is ruled by the virtues of loyalty and selflessness.

The novel, of course, would come to be called *The Hunchback of Notre Dame*—at least, in English-speaking countries. In France, where the work was first published in 1831, it was known as *Notre-Dame de Paris*.

Some say Hugo placed a fourth major character in his book—the towering cathedral itself, which still stands today on an island in the city of Paris. Notre Dame lives in the book as a personality. It is a friend of Quasimodo and a protector of Esmeralda. It also provides the reader with an example of something pure and spiritual, without mankind's imperfections.

For Hugo, a great believer in the dignity of the common man, Quasimodo was an example of the best that human nature had to offer. The hunchback was considered to be the lowest of the low and was called the King of Fools. Yet he always had inside himself the potential to become a hero.

It's only natural that Wishbone would put himself in Quasimodo's shoes. Like the bell ringer, our favorite terrier is a hero, too—always overcoming great odds so justice can prevail.

The Hunchback of Notre Dame has everything a good novel of any century should have—an exciting story with a magnificent setting and powerful, memorable characters. But it's become a classic of modern literature because Hugo was able to show us our own flaws in the form of Quasimodo—and ask us if we, like the hunchback, have the courage to rise above them.

About Michael Jan Friedman

Michael Jan Friedman, a *New York Times* best-selling author, has written or collaborated on 29 science fiction, fantasy, and young-adult novels during the course of his career. More than 4 million of his books are currently in print in the United States alone.

Yet, none of Friedman's writing experiences has been more satisfying to him than his novelization of the WISHBONE TV episode *Hunchdog of Notre Dame*. As it happens, Victor Hugo's original novel—which inspired the WISHBONE episode—was an early inspiration to Friedman as well.

Friedman still counts a number of nineteenth-century French romance novels among his favorite books. *The Hunchback of Notre Dame,* with its tragic hero and heroine, must be considered one of the greatest romance stories of all time.

While he has never had a hump on his back or lived in a bell tower, Friedman has always had a soft spot in his heart for the brave and generous Quasimodo. After all, as he learned long ago, heroes come in a great many shapes and sizes, and what's in a person's heart is always more important than the way he or she looks.

Friedman became a freelance writer in 1985, after the publication of his first book, a heroic fantasy called

The Hammer and The Horn. Since then, he has written for television, radio, magazines, and comic books, though his first love is still the novel.

A native New Yorker, Friedman received his undergraduate degree from the University of Pennsylvania, and his graduate degree from Syracuse University's Newhouse School. He lives with his wife and children on Long Island, where he spends his free time sailing in Long Island Sound, jogging, and following his favorite baseball team, the New York Yankees.